NO ONE TELLS EVERYTHING

a novel by Rae Meadows

ALSO BY RAE MEADOWS

Calling Out

NO ONE TELLS EVERYTHING

a novel by Rae Meadows

MACADAM CAGE

MacAdam/Cage
155 Sansome Street, Suite 550
San Francisco, California 94104
www.MacAdamCage.com

Meadows, Rae.
 No one tells everything / by Rae Meadows.
    p. cm.
 ISBN 978-1-59692-292-1
1. Women periodical editors—Fiction. 2. Brooklyn (New York, N.Y.)
—Fiction. 3. Murder investigation—Fiction. I. Title.
PS3613.E15N6 2008
813'.6—dc22

                           2007050801
Paperback edition: May 2008
ISBN 978-1-59692-294-5

Manufactured in the United States of America

10 9 8 7 6 5 4 3 2 1

Book and jacket design by Dorothy Carico Smith

FOR ALEX AND INDIGO

The girl has been missing for thirteen days. On the television, her parents make a desperate plea, their faces fallen and ash gray. The mother has a look of resigned expectation, as if she's about to get punched and can't avoid the blow. Of course she's replaying every critical remark she ever made to her daughter, every jealous thought.

Grace makes an inner toast to regret, and finishes her glass of wine. She's one of three left at Chances, the vaguely Irish bar at the end of her Brooklyn block. It appears the other two, a few seats over, will soon be leaving together. The sinewy young woman has a black serpent tattooed on her lower back. It keeps peeking out from under her shrunken T-shirt. She pretends it's not on purpose that her shirt keeps inching up, that she doesn't notice her new companion sneaking glances down to where the snake disappears beneath her low-riding jeans. Grace admires the move; the woman knows just how to play it.

The guy has nicotine-stained fingers and black hair that hangs over his forehead in a wing-like piece. He looks up for a minute and quickly sweeps the bar. His eyes catch on Grace, who smiles at him with half her mouth, hoping she seems mysterious, hoping her look says, come on, it could be fun. The corners of his lips jerk up, more like a tic than a smile, before he turns back to his tattooed friend. Grace pretends to drink from her empty glass. In the dusty mirror behind the bar she doesn't think she looks that different than she used to—pale skin, dark hair, angular face. But as her mother often reminds her, a thin face over thirty makes a woman look older.

Please make the professor call, she thinks. *Make him call and I'll stop drinking.*

For a year Grace has clung to the belief that the professor would pick her in the end, a wedge of hope lodged like a splinter refusing to surface. But of course he isn't leaving his wife, of course he was never going to. Last night he told her he's taken up Bikram yoga and he and his wife are going to couples counseling. He thanked her for helping him *figure some things out*. She wanted to tell him that he was a cliché but she knew that she was one too. And she didn't want to make it harder for him to change his mind.

"Jimmy," she says. "Can I get another one?"

Grace is drinking her usual Chardonnay. When Jimmy sees her walk in he pours a full glass. She thinks about changing her order sometimes, asking him with a straight face for a Cosmopolitan or a Lemon Drop, but when the moment comes, it doesn't seem worth it just for his amusement. It's soothing, this safety of routine. And Jimmy is her ever-willing co-conspirator.

She has lived in this neighborhood for nine years. First the artists dotted the Italian enclaves. Then, as in most gentrifying areas, the working families moved out of the brownstones and the hipsters settled in. Now it's space-age strollers, organic T-shirts, rutabaga gelato. She is glad, at least, for her rent-controlled apartment, her little wooden boat that bobbles atop the water, regardless of what the next wave might bring. Grace keeps to herself as the scenery shifts around her. Her old laundromat became a video store became a frozen yogurt shop became a pilates studio.

She looks in the mirror at the black-haired boy. He winks at her before looking away. Next to him, the young woman arches her back in a feline stretch before leaning forward with her elbows on the bar.

The TV flashes a photo of Sarah Shafer, the honey-haired freshman who disappeared. The sound is muted now but Grace knows what's being said. Still no sign of her, no word, no leads, since she vanished from the quiet campus of a small college two hours from the city. It's a picture they've used before, cropped in close, a disembodied arm around her slender shoulders. Something about her face reminds Grace of her sister. The light hair and brown eyes, the small, even teeth of her smile. Callie has been gone for twenty-five years but Grace wonders what she might have looked like today, a week before her thirty-third birthday.

"It's a shame," Jimmy says, turning from the TV, "about that college girl. Sounds like she was a good kid."

"Yeah," Grace says, taking a sip of wine. "They always say that though, don't they?"

It makes for a better story when the person is irreproachable, innocent. But then, at some point, the truth dribbles out—drugs or a townie boyfriend or some other unsavory element—and it all gets a little more complicated, a little too human. *A little too much like the rest of us*, she thinks.

Jimmy gives her a strained smile as he adjusts his pants beneath his bulging gut, a fairly recent addition to his physique. Grace knows he thinks she's bitter, thinks her idiosyncrasies are hardening into oddities as the years pass. He doesn't even bother flirting with her anymore.

"Maybe she ran off and got married," she says.

Jimmy wipes the bar down, shaking his head.

"You don't believe that, Gracie," he says. "You're just being contrary."

She smiles. She doesn't tell him that she thinks people

like to emote concern about something inarguably sad and remote, that it's easy to feel sorry like that. She thinks Sarah Shafer is not quite as wholesome as she's being made out to be. Maybe she's on a bender in Atlantic City, or hiding out in a squat in the East Village, or hitchhiking her way to Seattle with a guitar player. It seems romantic that she might have thrown down the gauntlet on a certain kind of life. That she escaped. But even as Grace thinks this she knows that if it were her, she'd be doing none of those things.

The newly formed couple down the bar murmurs to each other as they slide off their stools and head for the door, his hand on the small of her back. He looks back but his eyes don't settle on Grace. She may have finally crossed over into the gaping blandness of sexual invisibility, a prospect that is both terrifying and comforting. Age has worked its gradual and wicked magic to render her a mere facet of the landscape. She looks away before they are gone.

Jimmy clears their glasses.

"It looks like you have an admirer," he says, as he slides a napkin toward her. "For the woman down the bar. Zach. 233-3475."

Grace laughs and blushes, feeling both pleased and foolish. She wonders if Jimmy feels any jealousy, any proprietary twinge, or if it's way too late for any of that. He watches as she pours a little wine onto the napkin until it is soggy and the number bleeds.

"Hey, how's the job search going?" Jimmy's been asking her this for years.

Grace is a copyeditor at a weekly news magazine where writers encapsulate world events into short digestible paragraphs. Stories are decorated with charts and photographs, and analysis is kept to a minimum. She reviews layouts for typos, misspellings, extra spaces, overuse of colons, poor grammar, dangling modifiers. She envies the writers and feels disdain for them; she doesn't think they're doing anything she couldn't do. It's just that she got stuck. Her conversations with Jimmy about it invariably end with, "I need a new job." But by the following morning she's lost her resolve.

The hope of something better out there has kept her from shriveling up into dust within the padded half-walls of her purposefully Spartan cubicle. Its lack of personalization is her own stubborn statement that it's not where she belongs, that her residency is temporary, even if five years have already gone by.

In response to Jimmy, she usually says something deflective, but a while ago, in a flurry of optimism, she finally did apply for some jobs—a newsletter creator at a museum, a junior editor at a celebrity gossip magazine, a copywriter at a teen clothing catalog, a content writer for an online baby site, even a reporter for a local Brooklyn newspaper. She parted with those envelopes, one by one, with the flinty anxiety of calling herself on her own exaggerated expectations. She was hoping for a little luck.

"I sent out some resumes," she says to Jimmy.

"Yeah?"

"Yeah."

Grace smoothes her eyebrows with her fingertips, obscuring her face.

"Interviews?" he asks.

"No. Not yet."

"That's okay. Congratulations anyway. That's big news."

Jimmy goes down the bar to finish washing the night's glasses. Grace has watched his hair thin and recede over the years, as he has watched her turn into a wiry and solitary fixture on the third stool from the left. They pretend that they're not hiding out in this bar, each hoping that the other doesn't one day find a reason to move on.

She doesn't tell him that she's heard back from all but one of the potential employers. The rejections were pleasant and apologetic, but definitive nonetheless. They didn't say it but she knows they wondered what she's been doing all these years. She's banking on the one application still outstanding. As a kid she used to make deals with God, like: if you let me beat Callie in this race, I'll believe in you. Sometimes it worked. The past few weeks Grace has reverted to a similar approach with her job search, ready to barter her faith for a chance at a new start.

It's midnight. Her loneliness tugs, an insistent pull on her sleeve. She finishes the last of her wine, slips a few bills under her glass, and buttons her coat.

She sighs and says to Jimmy, "Say goodnight, Gracie."

"Goodnight, Gracie," he says, his voice warm and consoling, knowing and not knowing.

Grace waves and goes out into the misty spring night, turning uphill toward home. She wonders if Sarah Shafer will ever reappear.

Midway up the block, a scourged man in army fatigues darts out from the doorway of a closed drugstore.

"Spare some change for something to eat?" he barks.

The sidewalk is empty and dark. Fear rises in her throat and she keeps walking, her hands shoved deep into her jacket pockets.

"Sorry, not tonight."

"Please," he says with such desperation that she slows to a stop under the lamplight.

He has sores around his nose and mouth, a missing front tooth. But he is young, barely more than a teenager, ravaged thin.

"All right," he says. He is both strident and plaintive, his voice stripped bare. "I'll be honest with you. It's not really for food. Just help me out, okay?"

She reaches into her purse and pulls out a loose bill, a twenty, and hands it to him. He scampers down the hill toward the dealers on Third Avenue.

# # #

There are no messages on Grace's answering machine. The professor once had the nerve to tell her, stroking her hand, that she *simply lacked the tools* to express herself. At the time she let it go because she wanted to not be alone more than she wanted to call him on his arrogance.

She takes a few Tylenol PMs to drag her down into sleep and gets under the covers. She dusts off one of her well-worn fantasies in which she's browsing in a darkened bookstore, the light butter-rich and flattering, her face smooth and dewy. Her lips are deep matte red and she wears all black. She's in the Fs, and she runs her finger dreamily along the spines—Faulkner, Fitzgerald, Flaubert—looking for something she can't quite recall. And then the professor is there, leaning against a shelf of expressionist art books. He is forlorn—he thinks he may have missed his chance—and he is transfixed by her. She feels a taught wire of acknowledgment between them and her stomach melts.

But she can't even get to the point of his hand up her skirt because the image of Sarah Shafer filters in, asserting itself into her consciousness. Her glistening eyes and expectant smile. What is she haunted by? Who does she think of when it starts to rain? What does she want to be?

She was last seen leaving her dorm alone, past midnight, her ghostly image caught in four stilted, washed-out frames of security camera film. What did she do? Grace is more intrigued by the girl's possibilities than her own. She falls asleep thinking of her.

## CHAPTER 2

Grace waves to people as she makes her way through the fluorescent-lit halls of the office, but she doesn't stop to chat. The others in her department are amiable but she prefers not to join them on their daily excursions to the cafeteria or out for drinks at the bar next door. Pleasant but peripheral is how they'd describe her. Without her shell of detachment she fears she risks wandering the barren plains of ordinariness.

Safely at her desk, she drinks coffee and scans the paper for any news on Sarah Shafer. There's a small mention of her disappearance, noting that the police are investigating a promising lead. Alongside the article is the same photo that was shown on TV the night before. Grace wonders whose arm it is that mantles the girl's shoulders a little too tightly. She pictures a boy in a Greek-lettered sweatshirt who picked Sarah out of the freshmen facebook and then got her drunk so he could get in her pants.

"Hey, Grace."

Brian rests his arms on the top ledge of her cube and drums his thumbs. He is her boss, eight years her junior, and when it's just the two of them, his confidence tends to slip into adolescent uncertainty. He's always after something he can't ask for. Grace thinks he's intrigued by her aloofness. He thinks she is hiding someone interesting.

"Hi," she says.

"Hey. Hi. Can I come in?"

He slouches in her rarely used guest chair. His sneakers are big and purple. In his quest to be cool he often miscalculates with endearing fashion mishaps. He flips his shaggy bangs from his eyes and leans back, crossing his ankle on his knee. Not long ago he and Grace shared a drunken make-out session on a team-building cruise around the Statue of Liberty. They have never spoken of it.

"So we have to kick ass on getting the cover story cleaned up and turned in before close," he says.

Brian admitted to her once that he never imagined he would be a glorified proofreader, but he takes his job seriously because in no other areas of life are the rules so clearly defined, the satisfaction so dependable. Sometimes she wishes she shared his outlook. What she would never tell Brian is that she feels her job is a slow death, even though she's never demonstrated a particular drive to do something different.

"Come on. It's important for this department to show off a little," he says. He playfully punches her arm but then lets his hand drop.

"Hmm," she says, granting him a small smile. She shifts in her seat and pulls her skirt down over her knees.

"You might try showing a little enthusiasm, Grace," he says, deflating.

She has an urge to pat his head.

Grace imagines the thrill of quitting when she gets a new job. No two-week notice, no send-off party. Snip, snip. The joy of disengaging from this sameness.

"Okay," she says, suddenly feeling a tiny pang of remorse at the prospect of never seeing him again.

She likes Brian, and sometimes she wonders if she could really like him. His efforts are like little life preservers tossed in her direction, ready to pull her to normalcy. For now she prefers to watch them float by.

He jumps up from the chair and rubs his hands together.

"Strategy meeting at noon," he says.

Brian shuffles out, the cuffs of his jeans dragging on the floor.

She quickly finishes the day's assignments so she can search for Sarah Shafer online. There is a little piece in the *Nutley Journal*, Sarah's New Jersey hometown paper, an interview with her once happy family: dad an accountant, mom an elementary school teacher, younger brother a high school basketball star, younger sister on the seventh-grade honor roll. Vacations to Rehoboth Beach. Two cocker spaniels named Scout and Atticus. Sarah was supposed to have gone home to visit this past weekend. And no, there is no chance that she ran away. The family, the article says, has been doing a lot of praying. They have plastered the Long Island campus with fliers of Sarah's face, hoping for any information as to her whereabouts.

"Our daughter is a good girl," the mother says. "She didn't deserve this."

Grace clucks at this naiveté, as if goodness is any kind of deterrent.

Callie's death was the first domino and the rest of the family fell with unresisting ease. Sometimes Grace tries to remember the time before loss was a possibility, when they were four and not three, when she and Callie wrestled with every muscle in their girl bodies, each believing in her own justice, her own entitlement to more space in the backseat, more attention, more credit for her more perfect front-walkover. Before she knew that having no sister was to be her sentence.

She daydreams a scenario where it turns out that Callie disappeared, ran away, was abducted—anything that allows a chance of her showing up one day, her blond hair now darker, shorter, smartly tied back from her face, her body long and slim. Callie loops her arm around Grace's waist and they slip back into being girls again. "Gracie-Lacie, let's play kickball and I'm up first." For a moment the dream dissolves into memories of the old days, of how it was before it wasn't.

Her phone rings.

"This is Grace."

"Hi, honey."

Her mother's tone is always a little reserved, polite. Grace's shoulders droop.

"Hi, Mom."

"How's work?" her mother asks, not looking for a real answer.

"Fine," Grace says automatically. "How're you?"

Her mother sighs.

"I'm okay," she says.

"Yeah?"

"Well."

"What is it?"

"I'm a little worried about your father."

Lately a sense of frailty has crept into Grace's conception of her parents. They have been replaced by smaller, quieter, less able versions of themselves. Her father has arthritis and high blood pressure. Her mother broke her hip when she slipped on the driveway last winter. They are shrinking. Grace tries to ignore that they are, by most definitions, old.

"He's forgetting things," her mother says.

"What do you mean?"

"Getting disoriented running errands, losing track of what he's doing. He looked at me the other day and I could tell he didn't know who I was at first."

Grace feels the itching, burrowing roots of dread.

"How long has this been happening?"

"A couple months. I was hoping it would go away."

Her mother is quiet, looking out the kitchen window above the sink at the season's first lily of the valley, her favorite, coming up through the ivy. Her patrician silhouette and coiffed bob. A pastel yellow cashmere, perhaps. Pearls.

"You know him. He thinks he's fine. He blames it on retirement, his medications, the weather," she says. "I was thinking maybe you could talk to him."

Grace and her father have never discussed personal matters. They trade surface generalities and small talk like new acquaintances who have run into each other at the grocery store, volleying pleasantries.

"I don't think so."

"Maybe you could come home for a while? It might be good for him." It is unlike her mother to ask for help, so now Grace thinks the situation is worse than she's letting on. "It would be nice to spend some time as a family."

"I'm pretty busy at work these days."

Grace organizes a stack of old layouts, fearing her

mother can sense her lie.

"It's been three years," her mother says, her controlled voice belying her blame. "I just think it would be nice to all be together."

The guilt nettles even as it makes Grace want to stay away from them for another good stretch.

"Grace, he keeps talking about Callie."

And now Grace knows that something is very wrong.

Her parents still live in the white and stone colonial house she grew up in. Their upper-middle-class suburb, south-east of Cleveland, is idyllic from the outside, rolling and green with wide lawns, towering oaks, old homes, and a feeling of insular solidity. Kids she grew up with joined their dads' firms, got married, and moved into houses in the neighborhood. At the country club there are still men wearing pants with whales on them. Her parents never considered leaving, even though Callie died in the street right at the edge of their front lawn.

Her father worked for the same financial management company for almost forty years, from which he retired as a partner. He eats two scrambled eggs, wheat toast, and tomato juice every morning and he plays golf every Saturday, teeing off at 7:30 a.m. Her mother used to say she could set her watch by when she heard the garage door rise on Saturday morning.

A few months after Callie died, he decided that none

of them would talk about her anymore, that it was time—
and best for all of them—to soldier on. Pretend it was fine
and it would be, he seemed to believe. Grace and her
mother went along with it for years, even when it was just
the two of them. Her father slapped Grace once when she
was twelve for saying that Callie had ruined her chance of
ever having a pet by letting her goldfish starve to death.

The news that her father has been talking openly
about Callie is unsettling. Portentous even. Grace tries to
ignore the icy, creeping sensation emanating from the
base of her spine. But it won't go away.

###

After lunch, Brian calls Grace into his office. On his desk
is a framed photograph of the department, arms around
each other, in front of a race car at an off-site activity. She
is on the end, half of her body cut off by the frame. The
night she and Brian kissed, she remembers saying that
people play at being different versions of themselves at the
office. She wonders if the real Brian is even more earnest
than he lets on. She doodles a checkered flag on her
notepad as he talks, but then he notices, and she hastily
flips the page.

He gets up and shuts his office door before sitting
back down.

"So," he says. His eyes are green, speckled with yellow,
and crinkled in the corners. He smiles but looks away.

"So," she says.

"I wanted to talk to you about something," he says, playing with a paper clip on his desk. He bends the end of the wire back and forth until it breaks off. "It's not about work stuff. I mean I know you report to me and if it makes you uncomfortable to talk about this, please tell me."

Heat needles her cheeks.

"I want to make sure we're okay," Brian says, flashing his hands out, palms down. "Since the cruise, I sense a little hostility from you or something. And I didn't want you to feel, in any way, that I took advantage of the situation."

Grace turns her widened eyes to her lap.

"You'd had a few…"

So had you, she thinks defensively, even though she can't recall enough of the evening to know for sure.

"And being your superior, I didn't want anything to be misconstrued…"

She's annoyed at his presumption of authority, even if he is her boss.

"I'd pretty much forgotten about it," she says with feigned cheerfulness.

"Oh. Okay. Cool," he says. "So we're cool then?"

She actually gives him a thumbs up.

※ ※ ※

Grace is always eager to leave the office but once outside the door, back into the hurrying masses fighting for sidewalk space, disappointment usually sets in. She rushes home to be alone. Tonight, as on most Tuesdays, she picks up sushi at the place near her subway stop and a bottle of Chardonnay on the corner. In the evenings, the super and his wife usually sit on the top step of her building, waiting to ensnare in conversation whomever happens home. Tonight they are in their basement apartment, engaged in a Spanish screaming match, and she ducks into the building unnoticed.

When she opens her mailbox, a sense of crushing failure sets in before she even gets the thin business envelope open. She already knows. No interest, no interview, no job. All the best.

Grace unlocks her door and right inside her apartment plunks to the floor in defeat. She slams the door shut, hiding in the darkness. Her face burns for trying and she looks to the wine to wash it away, a cleansing current through her veins, carrying away the rejection. She is thankful for the corkscrew on her keychain. She takes a swig from the bottle and then another, welcoming the promise of the slightly tart and tepid wine that's now spilled on the front of her shirt. She opens the little plastic lid of the sushi tray and pours a dash of wine on each little bundle, as if feeding a nest-full of baby birds. *For you and for you and for you. And then more for me*, she thinks. A fire truck screams by and she drinks to that. A bottle breaks against the sidewalk and she drinks to that, too.

The telltale red light blinks on her answering machine.

"Grace, it's me. I know you're probably still upset. I wanted to tell you I'm sorry. For things. It's just best this way, I think. Well, okay. Good luck with everything."

How perfect. His message—purposefully left during the day when she wouldn't be here—is a fitting punctuation to their relationship. She tells herself she didn't like him that much anyway.

She is a rest stop, an intermission, a pause. At thirty-five, she has never been in love and she often wonders if there is something that has rendered her unable. A crossed chain of synapses in her brain, a genetic flaw. Callie was the sunny, outgoing one. She was light and Grace was dark. Hair color, temperament, outlook. Callie made people smile just by being. Even as a child it was already clear that she had *it*, that spark that people gravitate toward.

Grace was ten and Callie was eight when old Mr. Jablonski's wood-sided Dodge Aspen veered around the curve of Woodland Road. On that hot, hot August day when the brood cicadas had come up from the ground en masse and drowned out the other sounds of summer, when the sun-warmed tar was as soft as taffy, her sister's body bounced up onto the car's hood like a rag doll, coming to rest in the cradle of a crushed windshield.

When she thinks of Callie, Grace remembers the long flaxen braids, the impish cackle, the fierce longing she felt to know her sister's blitheness, to grab hold of it and swallow it whole.

#

Grace hoists herself up onto the couch and finds the remote control flush against the edge of the coffee table, this dependability one of the benefits of living alone. Even though drunk—*a bottle is such a lovely amount*—she doesn't want to miss the local news in case there are any Sarah Shafer updates. It seems, at the moment, vitally important to follow the story to its conclusion. She clicks on the television.

Before she can decipher the words, she sees Sarah's mother, her face collapsed in her palms, being led into the police station by her husband. Grace knows that look, turned in on itself, imploding. Despite her tears, the woman does not yet comprehend the enormity of the moment, still thinking that her child might come back. Grace's mother said that for years after Callie died she would occasionally wake up and for a few seconds not remember. Cruel bliss she called it, like it was the name of a perfume.

Grace turns up the volume. An anonymous tip led police to the remains of a body believed to be that of Sarah Shafer, buried behind a beachfront apartment complex five miles from campus.

Remains. It shouldn't be a surprise that she's dead, but its resounding finality settles heavily in Grace's chest. She had hoped against reason that the girl had gotten away, that she was doing something no one had expected.

There is a lightness about Sarah, a look of openness to the world that has always been foreign to Grace. She wonders if someone wanted to snuff that out.

The news has moved on to the weather, a week of warmth and sunshine ahead. Grace's head spins when she closes her eyes.

## CHAPTER 3

In the morning, Grace finds a story on her desk waiting for her to copyedit. A large picture of Sarah Shafer takes up half the page. She is laughing, her mouth open wide, a wad of pink bubble gum formed to her molars. How Callie might have looked in high school. Tan and freckled. At ease and happy. The photo is a close up, the strings of a bikini top around her neck, a strand of blond hair caught on her lip. The toast of spring break in Cabo San Lucas. Pretty, popular, all-American. Nutley High School's Sweetheart Dance Queen. The magazine couldn't ask for a better victim.

A smaller inset photo shows the parents, huddled against their grief, heads bowed, faces shadowed. Sarah's mother's eyes are closed, her face crumpled, her head curled into her husband's chest as if he might protect her from her flayed heart. Grace knows they will spend hours, days, weeks, imagining what they could have done differently, how one little thing, a phone call even, might have been enough to change the course of events. Their other kids will always be part of a larger story about their sister, and they will be angry with her for all of it.

The article calls it "a senseless murder," a phrase that lets people luxuriate in their outrage, puts them on the right side of good. Grace checks the byline—a writer whose prose tends to be overwrought and sappy. She circles "senseless" and writes "overused?" just to be irritating since it's not her job to suggest word choice edits. She knows what's next: "killed in cold blood." Another gem. She circles it and scribbles "find another phrase?"

But in the next paragraph, she's jolted out of her smugness by the report of Sarah Shafer's autopsy results. One deep stab wound to the chest that severed the aorta and another flesh wound near the left lung, both made with what appeared to be a short-blade knife. Grace puts her palm over her heart but its beating is muted by her sweater. She reaches under her shirt and bra and feels her skin, up under her breast, the rapid pumps of blood churning within a protective cage of bone. The knife would have had to hit just right to slip between the ribs.

"Hey, Grace," Brian says, standing in the opening of her cube.

"Hi," she says startled, quickly pulling her hand out.

"What're you working on?"

"Finishing up the piece on the college murder."

"God, that's so sad. She wasn't that different from us, you know?"

"Yeah," she says, her neutral smile barely more than a line.

"Kind of freaky. So anyway. I was just checking on the front-of-book section."

"It's finished," she says. "It was pretty clean."

"Oh, great, great," he says, nervously picking imaginary lint from his ripped-on-purpose jeans.

She looks at him in hopes of making him leave. She wiggles her toes inside her shoes.

"Grace?"

"Yeah?"

"I was wondering if you wanted to get a drink after work," he asks, catching her unprepared.

She blinks.

"Just a drink." He reddens.

She's jumpy, antsy to finish the article, which accounts for what she says next.

"Okay."

"Really? Cool. I'll swing by later," he says.

Grace watches his head bob away down the hall before turning back to Sarah.

# # #

The bar is a dark and modern midtown after-work place, loud with pre-commute revelry. Brian yells their drink order to the bartender, a skinny wannabe actress with fake breasts bunched together in painful-looking cleavage.

"How long have you lived in New York?" he asks.

"Almost thirteen years," Grace says, realizing he was about that age when she moved here.

"Wow. That's a long time."

"Yeah," she says, raising her eyebrows. "You've been here what, a year, year and a half?"

He nods.

"I arrived right after 9/11," he says. "That must have been an insane experience for you."

Not this conversation, she thinks.

"I hate how it's all so fetishized," she says. "It's a cottage industry. The justification for everything these days. A collective excuse."

"I kind of feel like I'm not really part of the city because I didn't live here then," Brian says.

"I wouldn't worry about it," she says. "It doesn't make me feel more a part of it anymore."

He eyes her, not believing.

"It must have changed you."

Brian is looking for a way in, but he's chosen a dead end.

"You know how it changed me? I know that if I had been in the second tower," she says, "I would have stayed where I was. I would have respected that vague authority on the loudspeaker and followed instructions. And now I know that I wouldn't."

She takes the last of her wine in too big of a gulp and whacks her glass down on the bar. Brian flinches but then he does the same thing with his drink and smiles.

On that sunny September morning, Grace left her desk with coffee in hand and walked down Seventh Avenue, straight toward the smoke and licks of orange. At Canal Street she watched in a trance as the towers burned and then fell, unaware that there were people inside. She walked across town and up to the East Village, sunburn blooming across her cheeks and nose, her feet wrecked in high-heeled sandals, numb amidst the people moving about, yanked out of routine. There was almost a giddiness, a mania to the chaos: *this is huge and scary and exciting and we're alive*! People stopped at restaurants for lunch and chattered with each other. Fire trucks flew down Second Avenue. Grace walked south again, through the choking air and the murmur of voices that tried to put meaning to the events, to the Manhattan Bridge, and she kept walking through Brooklyn until she saw Jimmy in the cafe across the street from Chances.

It was one of the only times she has seen him outside the bar. He looked smaller, more timid. It was strange to see his feet, and to see them in running shoes. He wiped the powdery ash from her shoulders. A woman at the table behind them looked out the window, crying. Outside, a group of men in paint-splattered pants huddled around a radio.

Next to his coffee mug, Jimmy had a pocket paperback of T. S. Eliot poems.

"I didn't know you liked poetry," she said, picking up the book.

"My patron saint," Jimmy said. "The bard of missed opportunities and lives not fully lived."

He hiccupped a mournful laugh. Grace knew she should have reached out for his hand then, but instead she slapped the book on the table and slid it back to him.

They didn't know yet the scope of the disaster, the deaths, the fear, the sadness that would shroud the city in darkness, the footage of the planes that would be shown again and again and again, as if this time they might see something different. The endless caravan of debris-carrying trucks that would rumble their way to Staten Island and the Fresh Kills Landfill. The smell of smoldering metal, fuel, and bodies that would last for weeks. But they did know that there would forever be a before and an after.

Brian drains his glass and the ice cubes hit his teeth. He winces and rubs his mouth.

"Ow. Okay, so I know that you're a great copyeditor. You catch everything. And you like white wine," he says pointing to her glass. "And you live in Brooklyn. What else?"

Grace wonders if this is a date or if Brian is just lonely,

too. She doesn't understand his interest in her. Maybe he wants to know why she'd rather sit alone on the sidelines than play along with everyone else. *It's by default, Brian,* she says to herself. *It's not evidence of an independent character.*

"There's not much to tell," she says. "I grew up in Cleveland."

He circles his hand to elicit more.

"I was born on the day the Cuyahoga River caught fire."

Brian looks sidelong at her, curious.

"It's the river that runs crookedly south from Lake Erie. At the time it was so polluted it was more like brown ooze than water."

He smiles, wrinkling his nose.

"They used to say anyone who fell in didn't drown, they decayed."

He laughs and wipes his finger through a water ring on the bar.

"What else about you?" he asks.

"Um. I don't know. I'm kind of boring. In college I majored in art history, but I can't tell you a thing about art."

"You really don't like to talk about yourself, do you?" Brian asks.

She shrugs.

"Pets?"

She shakes her head.

"Pet peeves?"

This makes her laugh a little.

"When people say 'impactful' or 'literally,'" she says. "Loud laughers. Being rude to waiters. Taking up more than one seat on the subway."

"Now we're getting somewhere," he says.

This isn't so bad, she thinks.

"Let's see. How about favorite color?" Brian's cheeks are flushed pink.

"Don't have one."

"Any siblings?"

"No," she says quickly.

She remembers Callie's funeral like she's looking through a tunnel. There is an echo to the sounds—the sniffles, the organ, the words that she can't understand. Her dad sat alone and she sat behind him with her mom. He smelled of alcohol. Grace wore a white-collared black dress she didn't like that her grandmother had sent from Saks for Christmas. She was there too, her mother's mother, Grace's only grandparent, with her hawkish nose and Ferragamo shoes, tissues up her cashmere sleeves, her arm a rigid fence around her daughter's small shoulders.

The air conditioning didn't work well in the church so there were two giant fans blowing from the back. There was sweat on Grace's father's neck. Her mother didn't cry. Instead she turned off the light inside and checked out, leaving her empty body sitting in the pew. Grace was afraid to touch her hand for fear it would be cold. She had wanted to be the only child, the one her parents would gaze upon with pride and love. But when she looked up at the little coffin in the front of the church, she knew she would be lonely for the rest of her life.

Brian has asked her something.

"What?" she asks.

"What do you want to be when you grow up?"

Grace wishes she were someone who could do this.

"Why don't you tell me something about you," she says.

He smiles and settles in his seat, happy to talk, ready to reveal himself. She finishes her wine and orders another.

＃ ＃ ＃

She leaves Brian at the bar and jumps into a cab home. Her mother has left her a message, but when Grace calls back, her father answers. She cringes.

"Hi, Dad."

"Well hello there. What's new in New York?"

"Not much."

"How's your weather?"

"Springish. Getting warmer."

"Good, good. Job's okay?"

"Yeah. It's fine."

"Your mother's not here or I'd hand her the phone. She went to one of her Junior League meetings."

Ice clinks in his cocktail glass.

"You can just tell her I called," she says.

It's the same conversation they've always had, each of them trying to get off the phone as quickly as possible.

"I was just remembering that time that you chased the monarch butterfly all the way to the Cooks' yard."

Her stomach seizes.

"That was Callie," she says.

"Oh," he says, taking a sip. "Why sure. I remember now."

"Dad."

"Hmm?"

He's in his den, she knows, in his beige Eames chair, with his octagonal wooden coaster under his glass, looking out into the dark, toward the cluster of maples between their house and the Millers' driveway where she and Callie used to play a version of kickball, using the trunks as bases.

"Are you okay?" she asks.

"I'm just fine," he says.

"Okay," she says.

"She was such a great kid," he says. "So much energy all the time."

Grace closes her eyes. She was the last to see Callie alive. They had been playing Marco Polo in the front yard.

"Dad," she says, with quiet impatience, frightened by his wistfulness.

"Oh, I know, I know," he says. "That was a long time ago."

Grace finds the remains of a bottle of Chianti in the refrigerator, left by the professor. From the smell she knows it has turned but she takes it to the couch anyway.

After a long swill from the bottle, she flips on the TV for the late local news, for any developments.

"Late today, police arrested 19-year-old Emeryville College freshman Charles Raggatt, Jr. for the murder of Sarah Shafer. Shafer, also a freshman at Emeryville, was found stabbed to death and buried in a shallow grave behind a Long Beach condo complex. No word yet on what led investigators to Raggatt."

A sweatshirt covers the boy's face as police lead him from the apartment, only jeans and Nikes visible. And large handcuffed hands. He is big, almost lumbering, and he stumbles before reaching the car.

The vinegared wine comes up in Grace's throat. She lunges for the bathroom in time to throw up pure liquid, blackberry-dark against the white porcelain of the toilet. It drips from her lip as she falls back against the tub; she spits acidic juice into a wad of toilet paper.

She wonders if Sarah Shafer thought she might die when she first felt the knife. She wonders when she knew.

CHAPTER 4

The next day at work, Grace avoids Brian as much as possible, slinking off to the bathroom whenever she senses his approach. She can't face the inevitable "that was fun last night" or "we should do that again sometime," the strained friendliness and sincerity. She spends most of the day hunched down in her cube trying to find out anything more about Charles Raggatt.

He lived at the complex where the body was found, a spoiled rich kid who was allowed to move off campus to the beach during his first year because money made the school bend the rules. He was the social chair of his fraternity. He drove a new red Land Rover.

"I didn't know him," a kid interviewed on campus said, "but I knew Sarah and she was awesome. I heard he crashed his BMW when he was drunk and his parents bought him an SUV as a replacement. She would never have been friends with that guy."

He supposedly had a $3000-a-month allowance, a 60-inch television, disco lights and a smoke machine for parties, and a penchant for boasting about high school antics. He was a finance major who was barely passing. There is no real variance in the tone of what is reported: he was an asshole who got whatever he wanted.

No one has spoken up in Charles Raggatt's defense, or expressed disbelief that he was capable of such a thing. In fact, no one admits to knowing him at all.

Grace wonders who would speak up for her.

# # #

Grace goes to Chances straight after work, telling herself she needs to go to clear her mind of the murder.

Jimmy bows a little when she arrives and pours her a glass.

"Have the job offers started streaming in?" he asks.

"Everyone passed on me," she says, waving it off.

"Oh no, really? I'm sorry, Gracie. I'd never pass on you."

He smiles but quickly looks away, corking the bottle and setting it behind him, even now, not wanting to imply a possibility of more than this. Years ago, before the parts they played for each other became intractable, in the middle of their banter he had asked, stuttering on the first word, "Would you like to go out sometime?" She had thought he was kidding so she laughed and then he blushed and then so did she and she said, "Oh, Jimmy" and panicked and said, "Sure!" too loudly, too late, too full of wine. He nodded his head but they both knew that the moment had passed, that the space of intimacy had closed over, filled in.

"Thanks, Jimmy," she says.

"Maybe you need a hobby," he says. "I hear knitting is making a comeback."

"As long as I can do it here."

Jimmy is pulled away by orders down the bar.

Grace lifts her glass with ceremonial seriousness, trying to forestall the pleasure of the first taste. She doesn't last long. She sips, and then she drinks it down.

Another of her father's old rules was that when he arrived home from work, there was no talking to him before his first cocktail. As a young girl Grace had such a crush on her dad. Tall and lean, his golden hair a little floppy, so handsome in his dark gray suit. His hands strong but refined; his nails, short and buffed. His monogrammed pigskin briefcase had been a gift from her mother, and its contents were an adult mystery. Indecipherable papers. A few pens in their designated loops. Grace and Callie used to watch him when he came in the door, whispering between themselves as he set down his briefcase, got a glass from his carved mahogany bar, filled it with ice, pulled out one of the bottles from down below, opened it— Grace likes to believe she can recognize the thwunk sound of the cork stopper of a Maker's Mark bottle—and poured the smoky amber liquid into his glass. He would sip it down a little and then top it off again.

"Where are my favorite girls?" he would say then, before even turning around, and they would come running.

"Let your father relax for a minute," their mother would call from the kitchen. But Callie would already be squealing as he tickled her. Grace would hang back a bit, smiling, waiting for him to pull her in for a hug.

The older man next to her at the bar orders a Jim Beam, neat, and she almost wants him to talk to her. It wouldn't matter what he said.

Jimmy pours her a new glass. She drinks and watches the soundless television above the bar. Attractive doctors getting it on in a supply closet.

The bar is filling up. In the mirror are animated faces, laughing, talking, elasticized. Jimmy is pouring pitchers, shaking martinis. A woman with brassy hair and deep scowl lines has joined the Jim Beam drinker. She nods as he talks. There is a formality between them—perhaps a blind date. Her armpit sweat is showing through her silk blouse and she keeps her elbows locked to her sides to hide it.

Grace glances at the TV but the doctor show is over.

"Gracie, you want a refill while I'm here?" Jimmy asks.

"I'm okay for now," she says.

She's making a new effort to stop at two and she steels

herself against her desire for another. *Two is fine*, she thinks. *Two is acceptable.*

When she looks back up at the TV, it's him. Charles Raggatt. A photograph of the arrest, his head uncovered, exposed. His face is pink and puffy, babylike, and despite a beefy, six-foot body, his shoulders have a slender quality, hunched over as if for protection, his chin scrunched against his chest. Mouse-brown hair sticks up in random patches. Not at all the person she'd spent the day reading about. He glances up and out with eyes that are exhausted, confused, almost myopic, without a trace of defiance. He looks like a child who has been awakened from sleepwalking, frightened and lost.

* * *

At her desk, Grace swallows four Tylenols with her coffee before she takes off her coat.

"Grace, hey!"

The spicy smell of Brian's deodorant hurts her head.

"Hey."

"I left a ton of stuff for you. Beverly is out today."

"Okay."

"Do you want to have lunch today? I mean with me?"

His face is mottled by the shivering light bulb above him.

"I don't know. It looks like it'll be pretty busy around here."

"That's cool," he says. "Some other time."

"Yeah," she says. "That would be good."

"Definitely," he says, his confidence restored.

Brian taps his fists on the top of her cubicle wall and retreats.

She flips through the new stack of page layouts on her desk for the Charles Raggatt story. The article is now just half a page, accompanied by his mug shot. They have a suspect and an explanation: a cocky rich kid, a pretty girl, a sexual advance gone bad. The sides have been determined and no one wants to be aligned with the villain. It will probably be the last time the story is covered in the magazine. The mystery is over.

Grace searches the small grainy photograph for more, but finds only the confounded eyes of a boy with a lot of secrets.

The article talks about Charles Raggatt's car, his failing grades, his notorious partying, and then something new: he is from Cleveland, one town over from where Grace grew up. His father is the CEO of a venture capital firm. His mother, a onetime Miss Ohio. His parents could not be reached for comment. Grace imagines them, prominent in the community, known for their annual holiday party. The mom is petite and tan, with expensive jewelry. She's had her kitchen and her eyes done. The dad has salt-and-pepper hair, goes hunting once a year with his friends, and spends as little time as possible at home. They can't bring themselves to speak in their son's defense. Bad for business. Embarrassing. Uncouth. They stay quiet and hire expensive lawyers.

# # #

"Did you see they arrested someone for killing that girl?" Jimmy asks.

"Yeah," she says.

"What a bastard," he says.

Grace has an urge to defend Charles Raggatt. He may have murdered someone, but there is something about him that she recognizes.

"We don't know everything yet, though," she says.

"Oh no?" he asks.

She takes a long drink.

"He's from Cleveland, like me. From another preppy, repressed suburb."

"No shit," he says. "I hope there wasn't anything in the water."

Grace gives him a small laugh.

"He doesn't look like the same person they describe," she says.

"Looks can be deceiving." Jimmy pours her another.

She shifts position in her seat, unable to get comfortable.

"I don't know. He seems totally alone," she says.

"Who isn't?"

Jimmy smiles a little and she smiles back. She drains her glass and counts out some bills, intent on making it home in time for the news.

The image of Charles Raggatt lingers inside her, feathery, shifting, like smoke from smoldering incense.

# # #

One of the last times she saw the professor, they ate dinner at a dark, brick-walled Italian place on Tenth Avenue, far from anywhere his wife might see them. Grace had sensed him distancing himself from her so she made the extra effort. She wore a skirt with tall boots—his favorite on her—and spritzed her wrists with perfume.

He had taught a class that night, so he was riled up, still in pedantic mode. He told her about a student who had turned in one of the best papers he'd ever received—insightful, well written, succinct—when everything else she'd ever done for him was barely mediocre.

"She clearly plagiarized. Or got help," he said.

"How do you know?"

"I don't know for sure. But it makes the most sense."

"So? It's not necessarily right," Grace said. "Maybe she was really inspired this time. Or maybe she got a babysitter and finally had enough time to work on it."

"The simplest explanation is usually the best. Occam's Razor."

He jabbed the air with a marinara-covered fork. Two red droplets landed on the tablecloth in front of her.

"That's reductive. It doesn't hold true for everything," she said.

"I'm just saying the odds are in my favor."

She bit down on the inside of her cheek. Under the table she gouged her knuckles against her thigh.

"Simplistic is not the same as simple," she muttered, stabbing her penne.

"Grace, it's common sense. You know what they say in medical school? When you hear hooves, think horses not zebras."

He sucked up a tendril of spaghetti and smiled at her. She said nothing more about it.

But it makes her angry now to think about it and she wants to tell him. She dials, but his wife answers. Grace hangs up.

She drinks well past her two-drink moratorium. She phones her mom but hangs up when her dad answers. She is restless, wound up.

Out on the curb, bags of garbage and recycling are piled in perilous saggy stacks. She fills a grocery bag with the empty bottles from the top of her refrigerator and carries the clanking bundle outside on her hip. The cement is deadening cold on her bare feet. She wobbles and narrowly misses stepping on a patch of scattered glass.

A group of boys walks by, two by two, razzing each other. They are tall but still adolescents, baseball hats under sweatshirt hoods.

"What's up, Mami?" one says, walking backward to face her. "Where you been all my life?"

He has a sweet face, with burnished skin and wide brown eyes that reflect the streetlight overhead. His friend punches him and they laugh, continuing on their way.

She envies their easygoing confidence, their comfort with each other. She balances the bottles gingerly on the top of the heap and skitters back inside.

In her bedroom, the light from the sidewalk shines through the blinds in stripes across the duvet. Grace lies awake and absently traces them with her finger. She wrestles with the things she knows about Charles Raggatt and the case, but they don't cohere. The story is only becoming murkier.

He has signed a confession and he is being held without bail. She wonders what it feels like to confess, if he wishes now that he could suck the words back in. She pictures his fleshy hands holding a blue ball-point pen, his signature precise, almost delicate. What if he wanted to give up his life? Perhaps now he can curl up in his cell and sleep.

Grace wishes she could do the same, but her brain ricochets despite the hour and the alcohol and the Tylenol PMs. Charles Raggatt. The telling thing is the silence. No friends rallying to his defense, no family offering its support. No one to contradict a profile that's easy to despise.

She gets up and pulls on her coat over her pajamas. It's warmer outside than it was earlier, a descended fog visible in the streetlights' yellow pools. She walks up toward the park, past storefronts armored with metal grates. A car service Lincoln slows next to her but she waves it on. A late-night subway train rattles underneath the sidewalk. On the corner, the all-night Greek diner glows safe and welcoming—there are other people awake—despite the dinginess of its greasy windows.

Inside there is only one customer, a jittery woman in sunglasses, emaciated in a cavernous UCLA sweatshirt. Crystal meth or mental illness or despair. Grace takes a seat in the booth furthest from her and waits for the old man behind the counter to stop reading his paper.

"Yes? You know what you want?" he calls out to her. His accent is Greek. His eyebrows are bushy tentacles reaching out in every direction.

Grace orders a vanilla milkshake. He doesn't smile.

When he turns the shake mixer on, the skinny woman jerks her head up, angry at the noise's intrusion. Grace smiles in appeasement and the woman looks back down into her coffee.

Grace wonders what threads they have decided don't support the neat story of the murder, what errant strands they have snipped away. *Maybe*, she thinks, *I'm the only one who's curious.*

The old man brings her a frothing concoction overflowing its soda fountain glass. She sucks it in through the straw, her head gripped by the pain of too much cold. But she can't stop. She drinks it down.

Maybe, she thinks, *I can look a little closer.*

She slurps out the last bit of the shake as the woman picks at a scab on her knuckle in the back booth. As she gets up to leave, Grace leaves five dollars on top of the check at the edge of her table, just in case the woman wants to take it.

Outside, the trees and grass emit breaths of green coolness. The sidewalk is empty, but somewhere nearby a can skids across the street and a car backfires. There is no moon for the fog. She finds a dented payphone at the end of the block. The phone is covered in graffiti but there's a dial tone. She punches in Brian's office phone number but freezes when she hears his recorded voice and hangs up.

A small man walking a miniature dog passes without looking at her. She waits until the jangle of the dog collar recedes before picking up the phone again. Grace calls Brian and leaves him a message that she won't be in tomorrow.

## CHAPTER 5

The campus of Emeryville College is tidy and traditional, the neoclassical buildings of the quad circling a wide lawn where groups of students sprawl in the spring sun. The Long Island school is small and private, with a quiet but decent reputation—a back-up school, drawing kids mainly from the northeast. Grace drives around and feels decidedly out of place. She stops to allow a group of girls with long hair and glossy lips to cross the street. They saunter in their slim jeans, unconcerned that she is waiting.

She finds North Moore, the dorm where Charles lived his first semester, and gathers her nerve to leave the car. In the entryway of the low brick building, in a glass case, is a map of the United States surrounded by photos of smiling faces. Pieces of string are pinned to connect the residents to their respective hometowns. Beneath the map in faded marker is written, "Welcome Frosh!" There is a blank square space where Charles's photo must have been. Grace puts her finger to the glass and traces it back to Cleveland, leaving a smudge.

She walks to the lounge, where two girls and a football player watch *The Price Is Right*, their lunch trays balanced on their laps.

"I'm so fucking hungover," one of the girls says, setting her tray on the floor.

She is blond but by her roots, a natural redhead, and she has attempted to hide her freckles with a coat of foundation and powder. There is something ill at ease in her forced languor. It appears she is, or is soon to be, the third wheel to these two.

"I have to go to section," the other girl says as she gets up, her small butt packed snugly in pink sweatpants, her dark hair reaching mid-back.

The football player holds up his hand and she slaps it with nonchalant confidence as she walks out, calling, "Bye, chica," over her shoulder. She is not worried about leaving the two of them together; she knows she has already won.

"Excuse me," Grace says, making a hesitant approach.

The once-redhead snaps her eyes in Grace's direction and the guy looks her over with mild disdain. His neck is the same width as his head. Grace clears her throat.

"Did either of you know Charles Raggatt?"

"Are you a reporter?" he asks.

"No," Grace says.

"That guy was a freak," the girl says. "I mean, like, clearly." She talks with her face pointed down, as if she's been told this is her most flattering angle.

"Did you know him?" Grace asks her.

She shrugs. "I saw him around when he lived here. But it's not like we hung out or anything."

"He gave a kick-ass party, though. Remember that first week?" the football player asks, nudging her knee. "He had a keg in his room. I was like, whoa, I am definitely not in high school any more." He looks nostalgic when he says this, like he has, in this one year, lost all vestiges of youth.

The girl studies her nails and picks at a piece of skin on the side of her thumbnail. When she can't get it off, she tries with her teeth.

"I've gotta motor," he says, standing and stretching. He picks up the tray left by the dark-haired girl in one hand and holds his in the other. "You want to know my theory? He wanted to get with the chick, she was way out of his league, he made the moves, she rejected him, and he, like, wigged out. It's not like they've been saying, you know, that he was some stud or whatever. The guy was a loser. Later, Amy."

When he is gone, Amy bounces her foot and bites a

new cuticle. Grace waits, unsure of what to do. She pretends to watch the TV. Amy picks up her tray from the floor to stand but then sets it back on her lap.

"So you knew him a little?" Grace asks.

Amy rolls her eyes to the ceiling, struggling. She looks around to makes sure no one's in earshot.

"I haven't told people this," she says. "But...Charles gave me a ride last week to the train station. That was probably, like, after he killed Sarah, you know? It kind of creeps me out."

"Yeah, I can imagine" Grace says. "Did he seem any different to you?"

"He was awkward but that was whatever. He said he was going in that direction anyway so it wasn't a big deal."

"So you two were kind of friends?" Grace asks, emboldened.

"No," Amy says aghast, clicking off the TV.

"Do you know who his friends were?"

"No. I don't know if he had any," she says. "He had a roommate first semester. John Kim. But I never saw them together."

"What about the fraternity?" Grace asks.

"Those guys just used him for his money and his car. He would, like, go and get all the beer or whatever else they wanted. He was their gofer. He even bought them a foosball table. Do you know he wasn't even really in the frat? They never invited him to rush. They're pretty much dicks."

A fresh-scrubbed boy with a girl piggyback gallops through the lounge.

"I have to go," she says, glancing toward the door. "You're not going to use my name or anything are you?"

Grace shakes her head. But when Amy leaves she takes another look at the map in the foyer. Amy Monroe, fair-skinned redhead, from Michigan. Grace writes the name in the notebook she's begun about the case.

She finds Charles's old roommate in his room with the door open, reading *To the Lighthouse* on his bed. He's Asian American, with small round glasses and a wispy goatee. He doesn't seem surprised by Grace's appearance and agrees to talk to her with a casual flick of his hand. She leans against the inside of the doorframe.

"I didn't spend much time with him?" he says with the upward inflection of not wanting to offend. "I was never here. My girlfriend lives in a suite in Franklin, where Sarah lived, so I was always over there. He had a lot of things. Material things. It looked like an electronics store in here. It wasn't really my scene?"

He pushes his glasses up on his nose.

It strikes her that this is a boy whom college has made comfortable with himself. Charles, it seems, was not as fortunate.

"Did he want to be friends with you?" she asks.

"I don't know. I guess? He wanted people to like him. He was nice enough but you could tell he was always trying too hard. He was always trying to impress people with crazy stories," he says.

"Like what?" she asks.

"Okay, this is going to sound nuts, considering the circumstances? But one night when he was really drunk he said that he thought his mind was disintegrating."

"He told you that?"

"Yeah, I know, but that was the thing about him, he didn't have the same filters that everyone else has. So it's not like anyone believed him. I don't know."

"Did he have *any* friends?"

He shrugs. "He must have some, right?" He runs his fingers over the edge of the pages of his book. "Sarah was cool," he says. "Kind of a partier. She's one of those girls that guys like and girls like? I just don't get it, why she would ever have been alone with Charles."

He points Grace in the direction of the dorm where Sarah lived, and on the way she passes a makeshift memorial at the base of a lamppost. Cellophane-wrapped flowers now mostly dead, votives, notes held down by rocks, a small, framed picture of Sarah dressed as Pippi Longstocking for Halloween, braids sticking straight out from her head.

Grace sits on a bench outside the building and watches the comings and goings of the dorm. Although the sun is out the breeze is quite sharp, the cold making the scar on the tip of her index finger itch. The whitish splotch takes the place of her fingerprint. She digs her thumbnail into the scar to replace the itch with pain.

When Grace was seven and her sister was five, Callie took their mother's sewing scissors and went into Grace's dresser, where she cut slices in her underwear and T-shirts, getting back at her for something Grace has long since forgotten. Callie, ever willful, her brown eyes shining with defiance, was going for the closet and Grace's favorite long dress, smocked and frilly, that she was allowed to wear only on special occasions. Grace tried to grab the scissors from her but her sister brandished them, using both her hands to snap the blades. When Callie caught Grace's fingertip in the scissors her eyes widened, but she slammed the handles together anyway, lopping off the pad, blood beading on the beige carpeting in small droplets. Grace stood there, stunned. Callie's contrite howling alerted their mother, who wrapped Grace's finger in the dress, the nearest thing she could find, to stop the bleeding. The separated part wasn't enough to sew back on so the doctor stitched the sides together in a messy bunch. It was the first time Grace can remember the cracks being exposed in a childhood that had been relatively carefree, cracks where the future peeked in, where life as she knew it was over.

"Do you mind if I sit here?" a handsome long-haired boy in a tie-dye asks.

Grace shakes her head and scoots over on the bench. He sits Indian-style, a biology book spanning his knees.

"How's it going?" he asks.

"Fine," she says.

Shade has crept over the bench and she rubs her arms to warm them.

"Right on," he says, turning back to his book.

"Did you know Charles Raggatt?" she finally asks the hippie kid.

"No, man. That's some crazy shit though."

"Yeah," she says, giving him a halfhearted smile.

Grace tries to imagine Charles here, his money the only thing he thought he had going for him. A boy who wanted to fit in without any idea how to do it.

# # #

College kids and old couples are scattered throughout the diner in town, its booths maroon plastic, its cake covers cloudy and cracked. The waitress, henna-haired and bulging out of her uniform, bustles about noiselessly in nude-colored nursing shoes. At the counter, Grace takes a place two down from a muscled guy reading the *Post* and tapping his foot. He has dark hair on the backs of his hands and he wears a gold insignia ring from some fraternal order. She looks away just as he checks her out. He stares. She orders coffee and glances over to dissuade his gaze, but he just smiles and lifts his cup in salute.

"How you doing?" he asks with a pronounced Long

Island accent.

"Okay," she says.

"What are you doing way out this way?"

"Excuse me?" she asks.

"You don't look to be from around here. Manhattan, right?"

"Brooklyn," she says.

"Ah, okay. Brooklyn in the house!" He laughs. "My grandmother lives in Sheepshead Bay."

She smiles weakly and pours cream into her coffee.

"Tommy," he says, extending his hand. "Tommy Toscano. Teamster."

He keeps his meaty hand outstretched until she shakes it.

"Grace," she says.

There is something surprisingly kind in his face, a softness in the mouth that she bets he doesn't like.

"So Grace, what are you doing out here on a Thursday afternoon?"

It's a good question, she thinks.

"The murder? At the college? I'm kind of interested in it."

"I hope they nail the motherfucker's ass to the wall. Excuse my language. Why do you care about that shit anyway?"

"I want to know the real story I guess."

He snorts, amused. "What, you don't believe what the

grown-ups tell you?"

She starts to sweat under her coat.

"No, I guess not everything," she says.

"You got a spark behind that cool façade, don't you, Grace?" he asks, squinting his eyes. He slides over to the seat next to her and says softly, "The word is he couldn't have her, so he took her. Simple as that."

"That's what they say."

Tommy's cologne is warm and musky. His thick fingers look like they could crush the white coffee cup he holds around its waist. His masculinity is so exaggerated he is like a cartoon.

"You know the craziest part?"

"What's that?" she asks.

"He drove around with her body in his car for like a week before he buried it."

"I hadn't heard that," she says.

"My buddy's on the force. Not working the case or nothing, but he's got the inside dope."

Grace nods and stirs her coffee. But then she doesn't want to miss an opportunity so she leans toward his ear.

"What I want to know is, why was she at his apartment?" she asks.

"She wasn't. Until she was dead, anyway. He killed her at the Econo Lodge out on Route 6. The same night she disappeared. They haven't released that tidbit yet."

This revelation plants a new stake, and the other elements must realign themselves behind it. Sarah went with Charles, or she met him at a motel, alone, late at night.

"They've probably made stranger discoveries in vacated rooms than a stain on the carpet. I think hotels do things to people. Allows them to do stuff they wouldn't do on their own turf," he says. A smile tugs at the corner of his mouth, like he has made her some kind of proposition. "I could drive you out there so you could take a look," he says, finishing the last of his coffee like a shot of tequila. "Before you head back into Brooklyn."

Her head swirls with the latest developments, which only seem to make the plot muddier. She wonders if Tommy knows more, but she also knows he's been playing her, and most likely he's used up all his lures.

"I don't think so," she says. "But thanks anyway."

His plump lips pout a little but then he smiles.

"All right, then. Good luck there, Grace."

# # #

It's dusk by the time Grace finds a parking space on the edge of her neighborhood. The early spring sun is barely holding on. Ahead of her, as she turns onto her block, is a girl walking with her mother who spits clipped angry words into a cell phone. The girl walks a couple paces behind, her posture sullen; her feet, which she hasn't yet grown into, drag. Grace reaches the stoop of her building but she doesn't want to go in yet. She sits on the top step and watches the pair retreat. Despite the girl's insolent walk, Grace thinks she sees something deliberate in her steps, and she strains against the darkness to confirm it. The girl avoids each crack, never catching even a toe on a line.

In the year following Callie's death, Grace's parents retreated. Her mother had her bedroom and her three-hour walks and the sympathetic kitchen tables of her friends. Her father had bourbon. Grace dabbled in obsessive habits that gave her purpose and kept her company. Most of these behaviors were internal and no one knew about them. They were games more than anything. Counting syllables when people spoke, touching walls, flipping light switches a certain number of times, not eating anything red or yellow. But then she started to pull out her hair. She would single out a strand at her crown at the end of her part, weave it around her first two fingers, and yank it, savoring the little pop of the root giving way. One at a time. A release she allowed herself when she was alone. The smooth patch of scalp was her secret and the whorl grew from dime- to quarter- to half-dollar size. It was her talisman. Her security blanket. It could be counted on to be there, to be in her control.

Most of the time she hid the patch with a ponytail so her parents never saw it, locked away as they were within their grief. By the time Miss Harris, her fifth grade teacher, noticed, her patch was the size of a silver dollar. Its presence so confused and sickened her that she sent Grace immediately to the school psychologist.

Mr. DiFranco was a short, broad man who wore his curly hair in an afro style, but because his hair was thinning on top, it went out to the sides in two bushy poofs. He was the kind of man Grace's father would have called a *yahoo*, so even though he was warm and she liked him, she knew her dad would have scoffed at him. So in a way, she did, too. She had met Mr. DiFranco once before, the day she returned to school after Callie died. He had told her then that it was good to cry, that she could come talk to him whenever she wanted. She never did, and had avoided walking by his office ever since.

The day Miss Harris sent her to see him, he wore a plaid polyester suit with an open-collared shirt and sat with his legs crossed to the side of his desk.

"Grace. How are you?" he asked, leaning forward.

"Fine," she said.

"How's it going at home?"

"Okay."

"I'm sure it's been hard on you, with Callie gone."

She shrugged and ran her thumbnail along the wale of her tan corduroys.

"Do you want to talk about anything?"

"No."

"Do you want to tell me why you're pulling out your hair?"

She shook her head.

"I see. Do you do it when you feel a certain way?

When you feel angry? Or maybe when you feel sad?"

Right outside the window the custodian was mowing the lawn. The smells of gasoline and cut grass mixed with that of the old coffee on Mr. DiFranco's desk.

You don't get it, she said in her head. *You can never understand.*

"You know that it's natural to feel guilty when something bad happens to someone we love and not to us. Do you think you're pulling out your hair because you feel responsible in some way?"

"No," she said without meeting his eyes. She had shut down long before this well-intentioned outreach.

"But you know the accident was not your fault, right Grace?" he asked.

She stared at him and traced the outline of his large hair with her eyes. There was a tiny part of her that wanted to open up to this man, so unlike her tight-lipped family, to tell him all that she kept hidden. But the urge was eclipsed by the safety of silence.

"It's natural, Grace, to feel this. To feel like you could have done something."

She hasn't thought about this in twenty years and she is amazed that now with the right trigger, the door to the memory has swung wide open, exposing all its contents intact. She gets up from the step and wipes the grit from her hands. She fumbles with her keys in the door, at once anxious to get inside to her bottle of wine.

What Grace didn't tell Mr. DiFranco, what she has never told anyone, was that she could have done something that day, but she didn't.

————

"He was a weird dude. Of course, hindsight is twenty-twenty and all that. He gave me Knicks tickets once."

"We were at the Saloon in this big group the first week of school. Out of nowhere he started crying and ran out. I thought he was just really wasted."

"I hope he fries."

"He was really sweet. He came in here about five times a week, always by himself. He ordered coffee, two glazed, one chocolate with sprinkles. He was so polite and always left a tip. He used to ask how I was, and that's rare these days, especially with the younger ones. I'm so sorry about it all."

————

## CHAPTER 6

A week has passed since Grace's visit to Long Island. She went back one night and posted a flier around campus asking for any information about Charles, which elicited a trickling of emails and phone messages, some epithets, one conspiracy theory about "commie academia," and a call from campus security saying such postings were against school policy. No one claims to have really known him, and even the gossipers, who wish they had something juicy to share, don't have much. What has emerged is a sad portrait filled in only with broad strokes from his eight lonely months at Emeryville College.

The fraternity has distanced itself from him, saying they knew him only casually. As Amy said, he was not an official member. He lived off campus at the end, rarely attending classes, by then rarely seen.

Grace sets about searching for someone who knew Charles before he left Ohio. Posing as a former student, she gets an alumni mailing list from his high school graduating class. One by one, she sends each person an email, asking who knew him and what he or she remembers.

"Hey, Grace."

As Brian comes around to the entry of her cube she quickly closes her email. His shirt has skulls printed on the front and a frayed collar, like he is some kind of rebel. It makes her smile. If she were a different type of person she might muss his hair. If she were a different type of person she might ask him out to dinner.

"Hey, Brian," she says.

"Is everything all right?"

"Um, yeah. Sure."

She hasn't done much work in the last few days and she hopes it hasn't become noticeable. She has an article due and there is more work she has ignored.

"Okay," he says. "Just checking. You know, since you were sick and all last week. And I haven't seen you much lately." He gives a nervous laugh. "So. We need to talk about the summer special issue? I keep forgetting." He twists to crack his back.

"Okay," she says. "I'll come by later?" She tries to sound upbeat.

"You should get out more," he says, wagging his finger. "You're always locked away back here."

The phone in a neighboring cubicle rings, as if to remind Brian that he has stayed too long. He half-waves before retreating to his office.

She tries calling Charles's lawyer, but as expected, he won't talk to her.

"No, Mr. Dubno will not allow access to his client," his secretary clips. "Thanks for calling."

Grace does a quick search for updates on the case. The D.A. has announced that Charles will be arraigned tomorrow on eight charges. Two counts of murder in the first, four counts of murder in the second, one first-degree kidnapping, one first-degree attempted sexual abuse.

Their story is taking shape. She just doesn't believe it.

# # #

"Jimmy," she says, "the usual."

"Gracie, for you, the best," he says, filling her glass.

The wine on her tongue is calming. She takes off her jacket and drapes it over the stool next to hers, just in case anyone gets an idea about striking up a conversation.

Jimmy leans over with his forearms on the bar, his eyes deep pools of dark gold, the color of scotch with melted ice. Like the contents of glasses she and Callie used to clear the morning after her parents' cocktail parties.

"Talk to Jimmy," he says.

"Just remembering something."

"From your face I would say it's not a good something."

Grace lifts her shoulders to her ears and lets them fall.

"My dad used to say, 'Memories can devour you if you don't look at them and let them go.' But he *would* say that," Jimmy laughs. "The old sonofabitch couldn't remember a thing."

"Nothing like bartender wisdom," she says. Her tone sounded harsher than she meant but Jimmy pretends it didn't.

"Can you believe I don't charge for it?"

He lightly pinches her arm and moves down to tend to other customers.

For Grace's parents in their Cleveland suburb, the seventies were the era of big-backed station wagons and light blue carpeting. Tennis groups and duck hunting. Valium and elaborate home bars. A consistent group of couples, some from the neighborhood, some from the club, used the weekends to overdo it with alcohol and each other. To Grace, the ritual of her parents going out was mesmerizing and exciting but edged in anxiety—she never knew the state in which they might return.

She holds an image of her mother in motion, sweeping into the kitchen in heels and gold bangles, her long, dark hair in soft waves from having been set in large curlers. She bends down to kiss Grace, enveloping her in her glamour and the womanly scent of her Joy perfume, leaving faint pink lips on her daughter's cheeks. As a girl, Grace was in awe of her mother's beauty.

One fall night, the air sharp with the snap of Northern Ohio woods, the party landed at their house. Grace and Callie helped their mom make her signature hors d'oeuvre: white bread cookie-cuttered into circles, slathered with mayonnaise and sprinkled with scallions, and then toasted. The girls set out ashtrays and filled bowls with dry roasted peanuts. They crumpled newspaper for the fireplace and stocked the ice bucket. Their dad organized his bar tools and glasses and bottles like a chemist preparing an experiment. He was merry in the way they liked. He was elegant in his suit, not yet smelling of alcohol.

By the time the candles were lit and the lights dimmed, the doorbell began to ring and the girls were sent upstairs to bed.

But Grace and Callie didn't want to sleep. They watched the party from the top of the stairs. Their mother swung through the kitchen door with a tray of crudités and flowed through the party in her wide silk pants and large hoop earrings, while their father smoked a cigar as he talked to Janice Livorno with the low V-neck and large, tanned breasts. Laughter got louder, bodies got closer. Grace was used to how her dad was drunk—she knew what to expect and when to avoid him—but other drunk adults were scary, slightly menacing. Callie didn't understand and she never wanted to be kept from a party.

"Come on," Callie said. "Let's go down."

"No," Grace said. "We're not allowed."

"They're not going to care."

Nina Simone, her dad's post-third-drink favorite, was on the record player, and the Wilsons from the club were dancing cheek to cheek, their eyes on other people.

"I'm going," Callie said. "I don't care if you come or not."

"Callie," Grace whispered, but her sister was already halfway down the stairs in her flannel nightgown.

Mr. Chenowith, who lived two houses down, swooped Callie up and spun her around, spilling his drink.

"Come here, baby," her dad said, pulling her onto his lap. "You remember Mrs. Walker."

"Lizzie's mom," Callie said.

"Right, sweetheart," Mrs. Walker said, with kohl-lined, half-closed eyes. She wore the shortest skirt in the room.

"Now this, Callie," her dad said, nodding at Mrs. Walker, "is a beautiful woman."

"Oh Jack, you're too much," she drawled, putting a new cigarette in her mouth.

Grace inched down a few steps. In the shadow of the front hall, there was her mother, wineglass in hand, staring out the window. And then Mr. Chenowith came up behind her, planting a slow, lingering kiss on her neck. Her mother didn't pull away. They moved off together into the dark.

Callie giggled and flitted from one group to another, dancing around, unaware that her father's hand was now massaging Mrs. Walker's ass, while her mother was being fondled by their neighbor with the large yellow lab named Louise.

Grace wanted to pull Callie out of it all, out of this scene that had gone terribly wrong. She felt strange, tarnished. But she couldn't turn away. A glass broke. An argument erupted between the Mitchums. Grace was nine but she had the same sense then that she still gets now, that feeling of *there it goes*: no matter how good everything can seem for a moment, it will sour before long.

The next morning, Grace and Callie were awake before their parents and they cleared the mess from the party into the kitchen—wine goblets and highballs and short bar glasses with remnants of limes or lemons or lipstick on the rims. They sipped from the milky remains of banana daiquiris. They ate leftover peanuts and drank cans of warm ginger ale for breakfast as they watched cartoons. Grace found her dad a while later, asleep in the car, passed out in his suit, an empty glass in his lap.

Jimmy holds up the wine bottle. Grace nods.

"You don't think I drink too much, do you?" she asks.

"Think about who you're asking," he says.

He pulls out the cork and hesitates.

"I'm stopping at two," she says, tapping her glass.

"I'll try to remember that," he says.

He pours. The glass frosts and sweats from the cold wine. She takes a tiny sip, wanting to make it last.

"You know the college murder out on Long Island?" she asks.

"Sure."

"It's not like it seems," she says. "I mean how it's been reported."

Jimmy folds his arms across his chest and squints at her.

"You know something the police don't?"

She balls up her napkin and throws it at him.

"Maybe. In a way. There's more to it than evidence. There's something about the kid they arrested."

"Yeah, he kidnapped and killed a girl. He's a shady character."

"It's not that simple, why people do things."

"I won't argue with you there," Jimmy says.

He wipes up a puddle of spilled beer from the bar.

"If he did it at all," she says. "I don't know. I don't know enough yet to figure it out."

"What? You think he didn't do it?"

"I don't think he's a sinister mastermind who planned it all out. People want retribution and they want a bad guy. It makes them feel better about themselves."

"You think he's redeemable?" he asks.

"I want to know more about this kid. I need to put together a few more pieces."

"Humans are a giant mystery, Gracie. If you get all the clues and fill in all the little boxes, we still might not make sense."

Grace rests her chin on her palm.

"Just don't put yourself in danger," he says. "What about the knitting? That seems like a better pastime."

He's summoned by a group of women in suits at the other end of the bar.

"I'll be okay," she says.

"Yeah," he says and smiles. "That's what you always say."

She doesn't tell Jimmy that she is ready to follow this thing wherever it goes.

 # # #*

A few months after Callie died, Grace watched from the family room window as her mother picked the first daffodils of the season in the backyard, her hand up under the throats of the bunched yellow blooms as she trimmed the stems to perfectly even stalks. In her mind, Grace pictured herself and Callie standing a few yards apart, her mother between them. She imagined that her mom looked at her, and then turned away, dropped her bouquet, and held out her arms to Callie. Grace became fixated on this image, on the feeling of being the unchosen. Even though she knew she'd made it up, the scene was cracklingly real to her, as if it kept recurring on some parallel stage. The thought so seared her consciousness that she would try to see how long she could go without thinking about it, forcing her mind blank, pushing away this vision she had created. It was too damning, and she had a sense that if she couldn't get rid of it, it was proof of its truth.

Of course Grace knows now that her mother loved her as best she could, that her obsession was born from her own unease, but it's never really gone away, that vague sense that she is a disappointment for having lived.

Grace couldn't bring herself to answer when her mother called at work earlier, but after her stop-off at the bar, she dials freely.

"Mom?"

"Grace. Hi. What time is it?"

"Did I wake you?"

"I must have dozed off. I was watching an old Cary Grant movie." Her mother yawns. "Are you okay?"

"Yeah, I'm fine. I wanted to see how Dad was doing."

"He's asleep. Today he watched eight trays of slides from when you girls were small. Such pretty children you were. I decided that he's just going through some sort of phase, your father. Feeling his age."

Her mother knows it's more than that but she's always in control, her emotions in check. Theirs was a household of silence, of close-mouthed smiles across quiet dinner tables. Tears borne in private corners. One night Grace's father arrived home hours late, but her mother pretended all was normal. She put on her lipstick and met him at the door with his drink and a kiss on the cheek. Growing up Grace sensed that it was more important to be slim than smart, feminine than ambitious. When the Taylors got divorced, her mother shrugged and said, "Well, she'd really let herself go." Grace preferred to stay out of view in the cool, obfuscating shadows. It was easier that way.

"How come we never talked about Callie?" Grace asks. The wine has loosened her tongue just enough.

"What do you mean *talked about* her? What was there to talk about?"

"She died and we were sad and we never talked about it."

"What good would it have done? Why does it matter now?"

"It matters," Grace says. But she relents. She lets her head fall against the couch and closes her eyes. "It might have."

Her mother sighs. "Oh, Grace. Let's not make this a big thing."

"No, we wouldn't want to do that," Grace says.

There are some memories that are tucked away, like the sun, too bright to look at for more than an instant, too powerful and damaging.

That August day twenty-five years ago, her mother was drinking coffee, watering her plants, dusting, getting the house in order in hopes everything else would fall in line. Grace and Callie were playing Monopoly on the floor of the family room and in the way of their mom's vacuuming. She told them to go outside and run around. She said she didn't want to hear from them until lunchtime. Their father was nursing a hangover in his den with a Bloody Mary, trying to soften his regret for how things had gone the night before. Callie tried to get him to come outside and play tag. She pulled his lifeless arm and said, "Please, please, please, Daddy," and tried to tickle him.

"Not now. Your dad needs some quiet."

"Come on, Callie," Grace said. "Stop being such a pest."

If only, each of her parents must have said to themselves innumerable times in the ensuing years. *If only I could have that morning back.*

Grace's role in the accident was something else altogether. She was there, the only witness. She didn't move, didn't reach out, didn't grab Callie's shirt, her hand. She had time to do something but she stayed rooted in the crabgrass at the edge of the yard as Callie tripped into the street, as the car didn't slow, as the body was lifted into the air. Grace shunned the memory of those moments, and for most of her life has refused to look.

She remembers them now in odd, still frames accompanied by the rapid click, click, click of a camera shutter.

# # #

Grace wakes up sweating in the late morning sun searing through the window, still in her clothes from the night before. At least she had the wherewithal to take off her shoes. She is already two hours late for work. Her mouth is dry and fuzzy and it hurts to lift her head off the pillow.

"I'm sick again," she says to Brian's voice mail, hoping her scratchy voice sounds authentically marred.

Today is the day Charles Raggatt will be arraigned, and Grace drives out to Long Island to see him for the first time. By the time she gets to the courthouse in Mineola, the proceedings are an hour behind. She situates herself in one of the wooden flip seats in the back. The old window doesn't close all the way and a spring breeze finds her neck. In the first row of spectator seats a Hispanic woman crochets until her son is brought before the judge on some kind of drug charge. The young man juts his chin out with defiant bravado. He has a tattoo of a tear on his cheek. The mother bursts forth with something in Spanish and the boy closes his eyes and sets his jaw. She says his name, Carlos, but he will not look at her. Finally, she crosses herself and then leaves the room.

Other than court personnel, there are only a few people left in the gallery: family members mostly, a reporter taking notes. Three more men are brought in— tough men, hardened men, men with violence and steel in their eyes—one for robbery, another for assault, the third for vehicular homicide. Grace fears the others can hear her rapid breathing. And then there he is. Charles Raggatt. A boy's face on an oafish body that seems to have swelled in the weeks since his arrest. His face is greasy, his hair matted. He trudges in, cuffed and shackled, wearing the standard-issue orange jumpsuit, led by a guard and followed by his short, bald, well-shod lawyer. Charles doesn't look Grace's way. He moves past the gallery and slumps into his seat.

She fights the urge to catch his eye and say, "Charles, I'm here."

## CHAPTER 7

You see his mouth moving but you can't make out the words. You have lost feeling in your left hand, the handcuff too tight. It's cold and hard against your wrist and attached to the chain around your belly. "In God We Trust," it says above the judge's head, but the letters blur like water spilled on ink. You've long since realized that your parents can't buy your way out of this one. The thought of them, small and disconnected from you, makes you angry. You're not just angry. You hate them. For what? For not understanding you and for always telling you to try harder and for being so providing and, well, nice. They are on their way to New York and you know the sight of them will make you cry.

The judge has said something else but you can only hear the jangle of your chains. You pick up one foot and then the other. You think about the smell of blood, metallic as it hung *in the room. You look down in a panic but it is only sweat that coats your hands now, bloated and pink and shiny like large baby mice.*

You try to tense your muscles to stop the shaking but it only makes it worse. The chains are getting louder. You are lonelier than you've ever been, and you can't remember ever really not being lonely.

"Do you understand the charges against you?"

The judge's voice cuts a hole in your brain. Your lawyer's whisper is cool and wordless against your ear. He is urging you to do something but you can't focus on what he's telling you to do.

"Say yes," he says, "tell him yes."

"Yes," you say. The voice is not yours at all but low and damp. You say yes again just in case it didn't come out the first time. It sounds like it originates from outside your body.

Your lawyer's cologne tickles your nose and you wonder if he can smell your oniony odor. You have not showered in almost a week and your hair is limp and dirty on your forehead. They have you isolated and they monitor you around the clock. If they only knew that you don't care enough to even get up from the lumpy mattress, let alone figure out how to hurt yourself. You wonder at the events of the last month but you want to say that it was all part of something that started in you long ago, before you ever arrived in New York, before you accepted that you couldn't shed the soul you were born with.

"Judge Richard Castiglione" the plaque says. You read it over and over, tracing the curves of each letter and leaping over to the next. You notice him now, for the first time. Although he is sitting, you can tell he is short, his head like a cantaloupe perched on a round body, his skin accordioned around his eyes. Now that you look at him, he seems more paternal than imposing, his voice firm but not mean. More like a father than your father, more interested in your fate, it seems at this moment you stand before him, than anyone else. You want to tell him how it was, how it came to be, how you arrived at this ratty courtroom in Mineola, unable to even scratch your nose, impotent against the churning in your skull. You're pretty sure he just called you son. Your lawyer puts his hand on your shoulder, warm and heavy through your jumpsuit, so heavy you fear you might tip over. He shakes you a little and you guess you are supposed to say something to the judge who isn't smiling when you look up at him, but isn't scowling, either. He doesn't look disapproving and you like him for it.

"Say yes," the lawyer says again.

All you want to do is sit down, even if it's back in jail. You are at once unbearably tired and thirsty and you wonder if you could ask Judge Castiglione for a sip of his water. You know that's ridiculous but you bet he would make the bailiff get you your own if you asked. At last the lawyer leads you to a chair, and then the other man, the one in the wrinkled suit who looks at you with contempt and waves his *long fingers around when he talks, gets up. His voice is a yell.*

"He planned to kidnap and murder Sarah Shafer," he says, but you close your eyes and tuck your brain deep inside to keep from hearing any more. He is the Assistant District Attorney, the one who hates you, the one who thinks you are a killer. That is not what it was at all.

Count one: Murder in the first degree.

You are nineteen years old. The boy you once were was overtaken by someone you despised even more. You can hear your father saying, "I just don't understand this," and in your head you answer, Neither do I, Dad. You don't understand why you were the one that was different, why you were the one that everyone decided was the odd man out.

Count two: Murder in the first degree.

Your lawyer tried to explain why there was more than one count for the same charge but you tuned out his words as they tumbled from his shiny lips. You are on suicide watch and the District Attorney could seek the death penalty. You laugh as you think of this now but you don't explain why you are laughing to your lawyer, who winces and then smiles a little, hoping to make what appears to be your craziness more understandable. If I am crazy now, you want to tell him, then I've been crazy for a very long time. But you seem to have lost the connection between your thoughts and your ability to speak. When you open your mouth, all you can hear is the sound of saliva sticking to your tongue and the roof of your mouth. You used to be able to control the messi-

ness better, but somewhere along the line it got harder and harder to keep at bay.

Count three: second-degree murder.

You found blood in the most unexpected places. A smear on the dashboard. Soaked into the tip of your shoelace. On the box of Tide.

Count four: second-degree murder.

Crusted in your ear.

Count five: second-degree murder.

You liked to hear her say your name.

Count six: second-degree murder.

Okay, you feel like screaming, okay, okay, okay. You are trembling. The judge's words sound like they are elliptical and warbling on a tape stuck in an answering machine. You wonder if you will ever go home again, ever leave the state of New York. But then again you don't really want to go back to Ohio, do you?

Count seven: first-degree kidnapping

Now that they are wrong about. She was not a child.

Count eight: first-degree attempted sexual abuse.

No. Not that either. Abuse is something you do to inflict pain.

"It was the most disturbing murder scene I have been to in my twenty-five years," the Assistant District Attorney says.

This you hear, the words chiseled as if out of a block of ice. That makes you, according to this man, pacing and jerking his hands around, the murderer. You wonder what he means by the murder scene. Does he mean the room? There was only blood left there.

Your lawyer touches your shoulder again and you wonder if this is his attempt to be reassuring. You don't tell him that nothing will help. You don't say, "I know you are being paid by my father so you have to try to be nice but you really don't have to." The chain around your waist is digging into your spine against the back of the chair. You can feel it and you can't feel it at the same time. Your head itches but you know not to attempt to raise your hands. Even though you are not listening, your body senses that the proceedings are coming to a close. Voices are coming into focus. The judge laces his fingers in a teepee. He is what—perplexed, sad, tired? Maybe he is just bored.

You hear the rustling now of other people in the room, a cough, a foot tapping, a pen clicking. It is getting too hot to breathe.

All sharp objects are kept from you so your fingernails are long and dirty. You want nothing more at this moment than to bite them. You ball your shackled hands into fists; your sharp nails slicing into your damp palms. Sounds are at once all around you, magnified, startling. It seems like you have bionic hearing. You identify a car door slam in the courthouse parking lot, the judge breathing through his nose, your lawyer's watch, its ticking slowing down until it stops altogether. You wonder what else is expected of you in this whole affair. Another yes? Maybe a no this time? The lawyer will tell you, and you're glad for that. Your eyes settle on the kind-hearted Judge Castiglione, but then again, you've never been very good at reading people and he might really be cold and spiteful. You hope not. You hope he cares about you at least a little.

Your lawyer says it's clear that you were not in your right mind, which in the eyes of the law means not guilty by reason of insanity. So in the best case, you will be declared insane. You find it a little comforting. It explains a lot of things over the years. It will show your parents that it wasn't a matter of just trying harder. Even with the humiliation that comes along with it, insanity gives you a slight power over everyone else. Okay, that's pushing it, you tell yourself. The trouble is, some of the time you don't feel insane and that is when, in the coming months, you will want to die.

"You have ninety days," the judge says to your lawyer, "to enter a circumstance of mental incapacity."

Circumstance. You wish it were all just circumstance but you know it goes deep down, to the bone. It is as inseparable from your being as the blood that warms your veins and collects in your chained-together, leaden feet. Your mind has been misfiring for years.

Judge Castiglione cracks his gavel down. You thought that was just something they did on TV.

"Okay," your lawyer says, "they'll take you back now. We'll talk soon. I'll be in touch with your parents."

You think that he'll probably be much more in touch

with them than you will.

You are escorted outside and it's too sunny and your eyes tear. You are relieved when the door of the police cruiser is shut and you can rest your head against the cool glass of the window. As you pass the donut place you know you might not ever be allowed another donut and your mouth waters and you close your eyes.

Up until now you haven't thought much about Sarah's parents and now you can't stop thinking of them. A wave of infinite sorrow makes you feel wobbly. The police radio crackles. You imagine she liked her parents a lot more than you like yours. You imagine they will miss her more than yours will miss you. Your parents, you guess, will never talk about it. Your parents will move to another town so that no one associates them with you. They will take your sister on a trip to Bermuda or the Caribbean or even Hawaii to take her mind off of you.

The car stops and you are back at the jail. The patrolman doesn't say anything to you as he opens the door. You don't move at first because you are looking at the sky beyond his head.

"Out," he says.

His hand is warm and tender on your head to keep it from hitting the top of the car. You feel like crying all over again for this kindness. You want to tell him that you are not evil but your jaw is locked like a vise and you are being walked across the pavement and his grip is around your

upper arm and you wish he would hold onto you forever.
Don't let me go, you want to say. Don't make me go in there.
But you are already inside the sickly green cement corridor
and he hands you off without saying goodbye.

The police discovered what they believe was the murder
weapon, a small kitchen knife, in a knapsack in
Mr. Raggatt's apartment.

"'Charles Raggatt is a faggot' was just one of those
stupid things kids say."

"There was this one time when as a joke someone wrote
a love letter to him from Hadley Jameson, who was the
hottest girl in school. He thought it was really from
her and wrote her back. It was hilarious."

## CHAPTER 8

It's three a.m. and Grace drinks champagne, a bunch of mini bottles, all she could get at the one open store down near the Gowanus Canal, amidst the hookers, addicts, and lurkers. It's a place she wouldn't even walk to during the day but she felt fearless, protected by her manic mood. One of the empty bottles rolls under her bed. She is on the verge of discovery and it makes her feel alive.

She hasn't felt this way since she was a girl. It makes her think of the summers of her youth before everything started to slide. When her dad could make her mom laugh, when she and Callie ran around and got grass-stained, when they watched the Fourth-of-July fireworks from their old army blanket on the golf course at the country club, the four of them, some fried chicken, carrot sticks, and cupcakes speared with little American flags.

Grace knows that she was the same then as she is now, too aware of longing to be carefree, too sure of disappointment to forget herself in the moment. But if she closes her eyes she can conjure her mom's luminous laugh, the rich, deep sound that changed irrevocably when Callie died, that grew shallow, then fizzled. If she closes her eyes she can believe that it wasn't her fault.

#

It's Saturday. Grace wakes up on the floor, her head under the bed. As she tries to extricate herself, she bangs her head on the bed frame, the metal bar hitting above her eye. She recoils into the deep, focused pain of it, closing her eyes against the stinging light of day. An overturned champagne bottle has soaked her sheets. *This is it for me*, she thinks. *I am going to stop drinking altogether.* The rug has left a red, rash-like patch on half her face and her ripeness disgusts her. Her stomach howls—she hasn't eaten anything since the bagel she ate yesterday on the way to the courthouse—but it quivers with nausea at the smell of her neighbor's frying bacon. Deep breaths through her nose. Six steps to a scalding shower. She stands with her face in the streaming water for ten minutes. She focuses on the words on the back of her shampoo bottle and copyedits them in her head.

Coffee helps a little and she spreads out her Charles notes on the floor. She imagines him in high school, believing against reason that the popular pretty girl liked him. She wonders if there is a way to track the moments in a person's life to reveal exactly when a course is set in irrevocable motion. She reaches back to the whorl of her hair where her bald spot used to be; the hair that grows there is softer than the rest.

The super and his wife are sitting on the stoop enjoying the sunny afternoon outside her apartment. Grace is hungry but she can't face their questions, their neighborly chitchat, their optimism. She is trapped inside, behind her pulled curtains, with no means of escape. She has never cooked a real meal for herself and her empty refrigerator gapes back at her. She cuts the mold off a nub of old cheddar and scrounges for some stale saltines in the cupboard.

She calls the jail and the clerk gives her Charles's inmate number and cellblock. She turns on her laptop. *Dear Charles.* But she can't type anything further. She doesn't even know what she is asking for. *Dear Charles, I would like to meet you, to hear your side.* No, that's not right. *I don't believe you were some type of predator.* No. She tries again.

Dear Charles,

I have been following your case and I am very interested in learning about you. I live in Brooklyn but I grew up in Cuyahoga, Ohio, which kind of makes us from the same place. I imagine that because of the unsettled legal status of your situation there are events that you will be advised not to speak about. I understand this. However, it is the rest of your life that I am interested in. Maybe we can get to know each other.

I hope you will write me back. I am enclosing a self-addressed, stamped envelope.

Print. Fold. Seal. She double-checks the address. She bites her thumb. Her heart hammers in her chest and she feels slightly faint. It is quiet outside her door, and when she peeks through the blinds, the stoop is empty. She slips out to the corner and deposits the letter, checking twice that it has disappeared down the mail slot.

#

On one of her many scattered pages Grace finds the number of Steve Daniels, a high school classmate of Charles's, now finishing his freshman year at NYU. He responded immediately to her email—she pretended she was a reporter from the magazine—and said he knew Charles. When she calls him she guesses from his breathy, conspiratorial tone that he can't wait to talk.

They agree to meet at a new NoLita bar that's all brushed steel and cement. He's in a tight T-shirt, jeans, and black cowboy boots, and when Grace arrives he is flirting with the strapping, overly bronzed bartender. Steve's hair is a lustrous black, closely cropped, and his long-lashed eyes sparkle with the newfound freedom of college. Unlike Charles, he is small and graceful, and she wonders what he's hiding beneath the immaculate exterior construction.

She holds out her hand and he kisses it like they are courting. She orders a club soda and he orders a Red Bull and vodka. His movements are mannered and theatrical. He plays his part with relish.

"Oh. My. God. So crazy, right?" he says as he situates himself. "I couldn't believe it when I heard."

"So you knew Charles?"

"I knew who he was. We had a couple of the same classes."

"But you weren't friends?"

"Have you seen that thing he posted on our high school's alumni page for our class? They must have taken it down already. Oh man." He covers his mouth for a moment with his hands for emphasis. "He said something like 'What's up Hunter High School! When not hanging out with my girl, I'm hazing pledges. My life is dedicated to keeping my fraternity number one on campus, my girlfriend smiling, and my Land Rover clean. I don't work but who the hell has time to when happy hour starts at 4?' Did he really think people would be like, 'That dude's so cool now'?"

Steve shakes his head and looks out into the bar. He catches the eye of someone at a table behind Grace and gives a barely perceptible head nod.

"Was he picked on in high school?" she asks.

"He was fat. A nerd. It was painful how he tried to get people to like him by paying for stuff. I mean, yeah, high school sucked. But lots of people get picked on. Lots of people don't fit in. But murder? Jesus."

Steve's mask has started to slip. He has not yet learned how to cement it fully in place. Time and practice will help. And denial is good. He sucks down his drink and touches his hair.

"Did he have any friends?" she asks.

He shrugs and gives her an empty look. His eyes flash and betray his affected distance.

"I think he hung out at lunch in the drama department, probably so he wouldn't get his ass kicked. There was this girl Kelly who ate there sometimes. She was kind of a punk chick. Or goth or whatever. She went to art school in California."

Steve pretends to search for an eyelash in his eye.

"Where did you eat lunch?" Grace asks gently.

Steve smiles but only with his mouth, then his eyes dip and he looks away. He looks chastised and his shoulders sag.

"Okay, yeah. I ate with him sometimes," he says.

She waits.

"We were friends by default, I guess. If you could call it that. It was better than being alone. I kind of hated him.

I hated that he was in love with a cheerleader and thought that she could like him. I hated that he thought he could dye his hair blond and look better. I made fun of him."

Grace opens her eyes in surprise.

"I know it sounds harsh," Steve says. "But I didn't want to see him make more of a fool of himself than he already did. And I didn't want it to rub off on me. We didn't talk about real stuff. We kind of didn't want to know. Talking about it would make it more true or something."

"Did you ever talk to him after you left home?"

"Nah. We had a fight toward the end of senior year. That was kind of it. I told him I didn't want to be his friend. I had a plan, and he wasn't part of it. It was every loser for himself."

Steve looks uncomfortable and unsmooth, still a teenager trying out a new part.

"Why did he do it, anyway?" he asks, his voice now quiet and small.

"I don't know that he did," she says.

He finishes the rest of his drink and vigorously shakes his head to dislodge the mantle of bad memories. Perhaps by talking about Charles as a distant character Steve thought he was creating a new, less painful past for himself. It doesn't seem to have worked.

"I have to go," he says, sliding off his stool and digging for money in his front pocket.

"I've got it," Grace says.

"Okay," he says. "Thanks."

He hugs her without pretense and she gets a final glimpse of the unsure kid he once was, the one he has decided to pack away for good.

"Thanks for talking," she says. "And if you think of anything else…" But she knows this is the last she will hear from him.

"Promise I'll get an autographed copy of the article?" he calls out in a singsong flourish over his shoulder, less to Grace than to the whole bar.

Not waiting for a response, he rushes out into the stream of bodies and the forgiving darkness.

# # #

"People are so sad, Jimmy," Grace says, swirling the last sip of ginger ale around in her glass.

"Not me," he says, cracking his knuckles. "My life's a laugh a minute."

She smiles. "Nice haircut."

"Thanks," he says, turning his head both ways so she can see all angles.

Chances is crowded and groups of young people press against the bar.

"Are you checking IDs?" she asks.

"Don't hate them for their youth," Jimmy says. "You were like them once."

"I was never that young," she says.

"You forget I was a witness to it," he says. "To Grace,

the early years."

A thin girl with a ginger mane knocks into Grace and apologizes with the gravitas of having accidentally cut off her arm. She has a genuine sweetness about her that Grace imagines Charles would have been a sucker for, while at the same time knowing that he couldn't possibly be that lucky.

"It's okay," Grace says to the girl, who gently touches her shoulder before going back to a conversation with others who look just like her.

What hope Charles must have had to believe that the cheerleader liked him, even as his life played itself out against him over and over and over again.

"Are you okay?" Jimmy asks, leaning forward to cut through the noise.

That is a question, Grace thinks. Even back in kindergarten she refused to smile for the class picture, the photographer a greasy man with thin lips, because she wanted to look serious, because she didn't think any of it was funny. She didn't understand how everyone could just smile on cue.

"You know, Grace, it's okay to talk every once in a while. We humans are social animals."

Sometimes she's not so sure.

"So what about this kid they've got? Your kid."

"I don't know. Maybe the girl was at the wrong place at the wrong time. I think he was a troubled kid."

"I'll say," Jimmy says, pouring five tequila shots for the

rowdy guys watching the Mets on TV.

A man takes a seat next to Grace. He is in his forties, with silvering hair and a Roman nose. Behind round glasses, his eyes are close together and watery blue. Maybe it's the fraying tweed jacket, but there is a slight air of gentility and defeat about him. He glances at her and catches her staring, then orders a scotch on the rocks.

Sometimes Grace would dance with her father. Not like in one of those sentimental commercials, where a girl in a pink dress stands on her dad's feet, but enthusiastically, with real spins and swing steps. The last time she can remember was when she was thirteen. And he was drunk. Drunk in the way that she was used to, louder, redder, wistful, his breath tinged with that warm antiseptic smell. Her mother wasn't there but they were in the kitchen and spaghetti sauce was on the stove. There was a John Coltrane record playing, coming from the living room, and her father took her in his arm without a word and grasped her other hand and held it straight out, with mock seriousness, sweeping her through the room until they reached the refrigerator, where he spun her around and then headed in the other direction. She laughed. She laid her head on his chest and let him lead.

But during the second pass, he tripped on the edge of a stepstool that she had left out, and he started to fall. She tried to hold him up, to hold him with all she had, to spare him the moment of his crash. But her will wasn't strong enough to support his weight and he went down with an awkward thud onto the terra-cotta tile floor. When he got to his knees he swayed a little, confused. To lessen his embarrassment, she didn't ask him if he was all right. He got to his feet without saying anything, and then retreated to his den.

"Hello," the man next to her says with clipped formality.

Grace has been staring at his drink.

"Hi," she says.

"Michael," he says, extending his hand. Small fingers. Short, bitten nails.

"Grace," she says, taking his hand. "Nice to meet you."

"May I buy you another one of those?" He points to the watery remains of her ginger ale.

"I think I'll have what you're having."

Jimmy looks hard at her but he doesn't say anything, setting out a glass.

Grace drinks it down fast and Michael orders them each another. She feels languid and warm, poured into her seat. He is a lawyer from Cincinnati. Visiting his mother. Or so he says. He doesn't rush to fill the silences and he doesn't seem to be trying too hard, which she appreciates. She downs two more.

"What kind of law do you practice?" she asks.

"I'm a defense attorney. White collar."

"Have you ever defended someone who'd signed a confession but didn't do it?"

Michael leans back a little to take her in.

"Uh, no. Confessions aren't really in my line of work. But I'd probably advise this person to plead it out and cut a deal. How come? Signed any confessions lately?"

"Just curious."

"Do you live close by?"

As she follows this man out the door, Jimmy catches her eye. He mouths, "Goodnight Gracie," and she turns away.

# # #

Michael's body is pale-skinned with sparse dark hair. A slight paunch is all the rest Grace can make out in the low light. They don't talk. It is a relief to go through the motions.

The professor rarely spent time in her bed. He preferred they had sex in his office, amidst his books and dying spider plants and the dated photos from when he had a full head of hair.

Grace takes off her clothes, not looking to be seduced, not looking for romantic gestures. His mouth has already turned acrid from the alcohol but she imagines hers isn't much better. He moves to her neck.

"What do you want?" Michael asks. "How do you like it?"

As if sex is a steak, she thinks.

She keeps her eyes open in the dark to minimize the spinning, and she doesn't answer. She encircles his back with her arms and hopes this is enough encouragement.

She doesn't know why she bothered. It's not entirely unpleasant, but she'll be left a little more depleted than when she started.

Michael's breath quickens. Grace doesn't feel much but she helps him along.

He finishes and pulls away. He has one leg in his pants before she even realizes what's going on. She appreciates his economical performance.

Was it as good for you? she wants to ask.

"Thanks," he says, zipping up.

"Have a good visit," she says. "With your mom."

"Yeah," he says. "Okay."

She rolls over to her side, her head perched on her hand, watching him maneuver his extrication.

He mistakenly opens a closet before he finds the door.

"Well, good night," he says.

He has already forgotten her name.

She barely makes it to the bathroom before she throws up. She slides over into the bathtub and feels the cool, smooth enamel against her body. She wonders if Charles lies awake at night in his cell or if he sleeps like the dead.

———

Nassau County Police believe a kidnapping and sexual advance led to a struggle, which ultimately claimed the life of 20-year-old Emeryville College freshman Sarah Shafer.

"He had this party for graduation and everyone from the class was invited. They rented one of those blow-up bouncy things. We all went as a joke."

"His sister was super-cute and totally normal. We couldn't believe she was related to him."

———

## CHAPTER 9

Brian picks up the phone when Grace calls in to play hooky.

"Hey," she says, her voice gravelly, weak. "It's Grace."

He sighs. She's lost track of how many times she's been a no-show in the last month.

"Don't tell me," he says bitterly.

"I'm feeling under the weather," she says.

She sees something on the floor and inches over to the side of the bed. It's a watch, a man's watch with a black leather band, unfamiliar. *Funny*, she thinks, *that he bothered to take it off.*

"Grace, you have to at least show up," Brian says. "I can't keep covering for you."

"I know. I'm sorry."

She rests her leaden head back on the pillow and hooks

her elbow over her eyes. He has some kind of techno music on in his office and even at this remove, it makes her feel a little sick.

"What's going on with you?" he asks, quieter.

"Nothing. Really. I'm fine."

"Grace, you can talk to me. I'm your boss but I'm your friend, too."

What could she possibly say? *You like me because I don't make sense, remember*?

"Maybe we can talk tomorrow," she says.

"Yeah," he says. "I think we need to talk."

She feels bad for making his life more difficult when all he has ever been is nice. She wants him to throw her another life preserver that she can let float by.

"What about tonight, after work? We could meet for a drink," she says, wanting to appease him.

"Yeah?" he says. "Okay. Great. You think you'll be feeling better by then?"

"Yeah, I think so," she says.

She reaches from the bed for the watch on the floor, barely keeping herself from falling on her face. It's a Piaget with a square face and roman numerals. *Thank you Michael from Cincinnati*. She slides back under the covers and tries the watch around her wrist, which looks bonier than usual, breakable in one snap. On its smallest setting, the watch spins around like a bangle.

※ ※ ※

She finally hears back from Kelly, Charles's other high school lunch mate.

"I don't have anything to tell," she writes. "But I guess it doesn't surprise me that Raggatt could be one of those whack jobs that goes postal."

Grace drives out to Long Island, the day humid and gray, the sky like rough cement. First stop, the donut shop where Charles made his daily morning excursions. The woman behind the counter, auburn-haired and white-skinned, is as soft and abundant as an overstuffed chair. Her nametag says *Charmane* and her eyes are pleated with crows' feet, warm and inviting. Grace imagines she gives a great hug.

"Hi, I'm Grace," she says. "You responded to my campus posting a while back about Charles Raggatt?"

Charmane's green eyes fall.

"Oh," she says. "Yes. Everyone was saying such mean things about him and I just thought...Well, I don't know. I thought he was a lovely customer."

A man comes in and orders a dozen assorted while yakking into a cell phone. Grace steps to the side as Charmane serves him with a smile. He pays and leaves, still on the phone.

"You know," Charmane says, "it's rare that people interact with me as a person and not just the donut lady."

She smiles and wipes the counter.

"You said he was always alone."

"Always. Charles sat there," she says, pointing to a small plastic table near the counter. "He put more sugar in his coffee than anyone I've ever seen. I just don't see how he could be the same person that killed that girl."

Charmane has powdered sugar on her lip but Grace doesn't want to embarrass her by pointing it out.

"Did I say how polite he was? Always 'please' and 'thank you.' He would clear his table and wipe it with a napkin even when there was nothing there to clean up."

"Did you see him during the time the girl was missing?" Grace asks.

Charmane looks at her for a moment and then shakes her head.

"One day he just stopped coming in. I remember wondering where he was. I wanted to ask him if he knew her. I guess it hurt my feelings a little that he never came back. There are some things you count on."

She is over forty, but Grace senses she may have entertained romantic thoughts about Charles. They had a certain rapport, and maybe he came to this donut shop every day because of her.

"Did he ever talk about himself?" Grace asks.

Charmane thinks for a moment, deciding whether to tell her anything.

"He said once that his parents were dead. That I remember. Died in some sort of sailing accident. He was vague about the whole thing."

"Oh," Grace says. "His parents actually live in Cleveland, I think. Maybe he wasn't very close with them."

She spins her new watch around her wrist to avoid seeing the other woman's disappointment.

Charmane moves a row of jelly donuts to the front of a tray and sniffs. She doesn't want to hear any more.

"You could use a little meat on your bones," Charmane says. Take a few with you."

She puts three donuts—two glazed, one chocolate with sprinkles, the same order Charles used to get—in a white bag and hands it to Grace, waving away her money.

Grace drives slowly by the diner near campus, hoping to see the teamster again, wishing now that she had taken him up on his offer to take her to the motel. But he isn't at the counter. She drives south past the gas stations and a crumbling mall, and west under the highway and into the next town, Hickton, noticeably seedier than Emeryville.

Kingston Road turns into Route 6, and after a couple of miles, she comes upon the Econo Lodge surrounded by scraggly trees, a few low-slung ranch-style houses, and little else. The day has darkened and as she pulls into the lot the rain starts. Sporadic drops turn to pounding sheets and she turns her wipers on high, taking in the rusting aluminum siding of the shabby, loveless motel, its neon sign visible in the storm. No wonder the night manager didn't report anything. No wonder he didn't think much of a sticky dark stain matting down the musty carpet.

A few cars are parked on the side of the two-story building but most of the rooms appear unoccupied. Grace runs through the rain to the chilly office that smells of coconut air freshener. The counter is pink Formica, and there are two mauve plastic chairs pulled up to a small coffee table fanned with brochures about all the shopping adventures Long Island has to offer. A TV babbles from somewhere in back but no one comes out. $49.99 a night. HBO. A safe in the office for valuables. She rings the bell.

A young man emerges. He's thin, almost dainty, his brown skin shiny, his eyelashes curling up from his almond eyes. His uniform top is black with gold buttons and it's too big around his neck.

"You would like a room, miss?" he asks, with a smile of long white teeth.

"Hi," she says. "Is there a chance you were working the night of April 23rd?"

"Listen. I can't talk about it."

"You were here then?"

"You can direct all inquiries to my employer."

"I won't use your name. I'm just looking to find some things out."

"I told the police everything."

"Do you remember Charles Raggatt?"

"I checked him in in the evening. He was alone. When he checked out, he was still alone."

"Did he say anything when he checked out?"

He looks at the door and shakes his head.

"I can't talk to you," he says.

"Anything?" she asks.

"He said that he cut himself, okay? He said he'd had an accident and that I could use his credit card to hire a cleaning service."

"And you believed him?"

"Yes, I believed him," he yells, slapping his palm against the counter, startling her. "I believed him enough to take care of it. What do you think, I knew he'd done this crazy shit in there and I didn't do anything about it? Do you think my boss wants to know every time the cleaning woman finds something?"

"I'm sorry," she says.

"He was nice. That's what I remember," he says, his voice back in control. "He said he was just passing through and wanted to sleep. He seemed normal. And he had an American Express gold card. It's not often I get one of those here."

# # #

Grace stops in the parking lot of a liquor store near the highway. She wants wine to calm her nervous heart and shaky hands, but she sits in her car and hangs onto the wheel, watching the rain, testing her will not to falter. Focus. Sarah Shafer ended up at the hotel, too, after Charles had checked in. If he were going to drug and abduct her as they claim, why would he have risked a public place?

Her jeans are soaked and stuck to her thighs. Her mascara has left deep smudges under her eyes. She wolfs down two of the donuts, chocolate glaze coating her mouth and sticking to the corners of her lips. She checks the time but her new watch has already stopped working.

# # #

Brian sits at a dingy place in the East Village that has two pinball machines and a pool table. Despite the city smoking ban, the kids smoke openly, ashing into bottle caps and soda cans. He's wearing his purple sneakers again, his laces tied in childlike double knots, and when Grace walks in, she catches him turning his eyes from the door to hide his eagerness.

"I thought you might not show," Brian says.

"Give me a little credit," she says.

She looks around and feels old; the bartender, with her pierced lip and her jet-black, baby-doll bangs, looks barely old enough to drive.

When Brian orders Grace gets a whiff of mint, which means he stopped home to brush his teeth before coming here. He hasn't given up on her yet. She orders a Coke.

He takes her in, then sips his beer.

"So," he says.

She waits, glancing down at the chocolate donut stain on her chest.

"Are you okay? I mean, don't take this the wrong way or anything, but you don't look so good," he says.

She takes a long slug, finishing half her soda. She can't bring herself to say anything to help him out. It's more energy than she can muster. She knows she is daring him to cut her loose.

"Grace. I'm just worried. Are you sick? Are you doing drugs? Are you depressed? What? You can tell me."

"I know," she says. "Thanks for your concern. But I'm okay. Really. I'm distracted. Tired. Maybe I just need a vacation."

"I hadn't thought of that," he says. "You should take some time off. You never use your vacation days."

"Maybe a trip to Bermuda would be just the thing."

He smiles.

"Nice watch," he says, eyeing her wrist.

"I think I broke it by wearing it in the rain."

"Let me see it for a minute?"

She slides it over her hand without unbuckling it and hands it to him.

"You just have to wind it. See?"

He holds it out to her and she pulls it and him closer. She kisses him. His lips, soft and young. And she goes in for more.

"No. Grace," he says, his hand pushing her back by her shoulder. "Sorry."

He is red, even in this shitty light she can see his neck splotch, his cheeks blaze.

She reaches for her purse on the floor and laughs in a

lame attempt to make it right. She shrugs with exaggerated girlishness, embarrassing herself even further. She feels sorry for him and for herself. She forces the tears back.

"It's okay," he says, rising. "You don't have to go."

"I do," she says. "But I'll see you tomorrow, okay? And I'll be on time."

The rain abates to a soft mist as she stumbles home, slipping on the wet sidewalk. In the mailbox, amidst the junk mail and utility bills, is an envelope addressed to her in her own hand. Her stomach plummets. By the time she gets the door open and finds the light she is afraid to open it. It could be a Xeroxed form from the jail saying that the prisoner did not accept her letter, that he has refused all future correspondence. Or it could be the beginning.

She tears the seal of the envelope. The unimaginably neat black print hovers just above the lines of the paper. And with a deep breath, she starts.

> Dear Grace,
>
> I wish I had a computer to write this letter. I hope that my handwriting isn't too bad. I'm under mental observation so I'm not allowed normal pens. I have to write with the bendable inside tube. If you've ever taken a pen apart you know what I'm talking about.

Thank you for writing to me. Yours is the first letter that didn't include phrases like: "you deserve the chair," "rot in hell," and "enjoy the rest of your life in prison."

You were right that I can't discuss the case. But I can tell you that much of what the news reported is not the truth. Maybe one day I can share more with you, but there isn't a lot about it I can tell you now.

I can't begin to imagine the pain and the suffering that Sarah's family is going through. I think about them all the time. I hope one day I can show them that I'm not the monster I'm being made out to be. But I don't think they'll want to talk to me anytime soon.

So I will end this letter now. I hope to hear from you again.

Sincerely,
Charles T. Raggatt

P.S. There are many questions that I probably can answer, you just have to ask.

#

It's midnight and Grace lies on the floor, staring at the ceiling, unable to move even though she has had to pee for an hour. When she finally gets up, she sees the light on her message machine blinking, which she hadn't noticed in all the excitement. No doubt Brian trying to make her feel better. She presses play on the way back from the bathroom, peels off her clothes, and falls into bed, ready to bury her head under her pillow.

"Grace. It's Mom. Where are you? Call as soon as you get this. It's your father. He's had a stroke."

Grace bolts upright. She grabs her pillow and hurls it across the room, knocking over a glass of water on her dresser.

She calls home. Her mother answers on the first ring.

## CHAPTER 10

Your cell door buzzes, announcing the guard's entrance.

"Raggatt, you alive in here?"

This is a little joke, since he is the one to monitor you for suicidal ingenuity. He also brings you a little paper cup with your pill in it that he watches you take, then inspects under your tongue so you can't stockpile for an overdose. They're giving you something so you don't off yourself. They've taken everything you could possibly construe as having an ulterior use from your cell. Instead of a mirror you have a semi-reflective sheet of metal bolted to the wall, which makes for some uneven shaving with your safety razor.

The guard looks at you with pity.

"If you want to shower today, be ready at two and some-one'll take you. Our shifts are screwed up."

He leaves while he's talking, and the door clacks closed

and locks with all its satisfying finality. For the briefest moment there is silence.

It's eight a.m. You have reserved an old People with Julia Roberts on the cover for the day's entertainment, then lunch, then a shower, then perhaps a visit from your lawyer. You write the day's plan down on a piece of loose-leaf notebook paper (no spirals or binders allowed). Then you write: wake up, take pill, breathe—all of which you then cross out—then: try to sleep, pee, eat. You add at the bottom 'find God,' and laugh, but you're only laughing because you're supposed to laugh at something like that, like a character would do in a movie. But there's no camera here and you don't think it's funny anyway. So you stop and drag your pen over and over and over it.

"How are you feeling today?" your attorney asks.

He wears a pinkie ring and he drives a gold Lexus–or so he tells you. He seems to like you better lately. Well, you know he doesn't like you but he is less fearful of you, less disgusted. He thinks you seem a little more in control.

"Fine," you say.

He's all business. You wonder how much he makes for this visit, how much Charles Sr. shells out to have him drive here to ask you how you are. In the fluorescent light of the visiting room, you can see stray hairs on his smooth head and you make yourself look elsewhere. The hairs are there, though, in your periphery when you look at him and when *you close your eyes.*

"We're conferencing Thursday to try to work out a tentative proposal for a trial date. The longer we wait the better. The further out from media accounts the better. Did you see the doctor this week?"

"Yeah," you say. "I see him every week."

Dubno looks different now than he did to you at first. Smaller. Less powerful. He doesn't ask much of you other than to believe that you are mentally ill, for the good of the case. You know he believes you did it though he's never asked you. But to be fair, you know it doesn't matter to him or his job. He says he believes you were sick, and that makes you not entirely culpable.

"Good. His testimony will be important," he says.

On the yellow legal pad that rests on his crossed leg, he scratches down notes even though you are not saying anything. The letters he makes are long and narrow and the lines that form them don't connect. The words he writes float on the page and when you stare at them they start to move, as if to rearrange themselves.

"We're weak on people who can testify on your behalf. None of the boys from the fraternity. We've contacted all of them."

Even though you knew this, it hurts to hear.

"She would have," you say.

"Who would have what?" he asks.

"Sarah." You laugh silently as you cry. "She would have

testified on my behalf."

Inside your skull you can feel the battle between self-preservation and the powerful beast of your memory. If you look closely you think you can still see blood under your fingernails.

"Okay, okay. Take it easy." Dubno reaches his hand to touch your arm, then stops and rubs his chin instead.

You lean back to make him feel better, to make him feel further away from you. The suppressants go to work and blanket the bubbling crevices of your brain.

He underlines something three times then checks his watch.

"Charles. Your parents want you in treatment, not in prison. This is only going to happen if we win. Insanity is not an easy thing to get a jury to decide on."

The stray hairs on his head flutter, though you feel no breeze in the dead air of the room. You wonder if he senses with them, like antennae. You want to smooth them down.

"They'll be here next week?" he asks.

"Who?"

"Your parents," he says, trying to look like it's not weird that you didn't know to whom he was referring.

"Oh. Yeah," you say.

Kathy and Charles Sr., dressed up, so painfully out of their element in the jail. They'll look like forms cut from plywood when they stand in the vestibule waiting for your arrival, his arm around her waist like they are posing for a formal portrait. Your mother, as always, in freshly applied coral lipstick. She has been wearing the same shade all your life.

"I talked to your father last night about some particulars," Dubno says.

He taps his notepad on the table as if to straighten loose papers, to announce the end of his visit.

You wonder if he thinks you are awful. But you also wonder if it makes him feel better to know you, to lessen his own guilt for the bad things he has probably done.

"Okay, then," Dubno says, "We'll talk soon."

Particulars. The weeks before your arrest are proving the most problematic to your defense. You were your other self then. The Charles who was separated from you, leaving a space, an airshaft, between you and your actions. When you drove around the next day, certainly you were aware of a presence, a heaviness to the smell inside the car, a sense deep in your bones that somewhere in the corroded folds of your cerebral cortex lay the horror, the reason why you refused to look at the tarp-covered mound in the trunk.

With your eyes you trace the ridges and pits of the cement ceiling of your cell, back and forth. It is like when you were little and you pretended the ceiling was the floor and you had to step over the chandelier, which bloomed up like a huge bejeweled flower.

## CHAPTER 11

The A train car is fairly full, but Grace gets a seat next to an empty one and pulls her suitcase close. Across from her are two junkies wrapped in mangy army coats despite the warmth of the afternoon.

"I love spring on the subway," one says.

"How come?" the other answers.

"Because of all the nipples. Especially when it rains," he says.

His laugh gets tangled in a phlegmy cough.

"Right on, man, right on. It's paradise."

Grace crosses her arms across her chest and looks at the floor. A leaking can of root beer rolls by, only to get stuck on a wad of neon green gum. It's humid and rank and the open window only lets in the dirty, subterranean air. Her stomach muscles strain to hold everything down.

The junkies nod off like lovebirds, one's head nestled on the other's shoulder.

###

She is so small. That's the first thought Grace has when she sees her mother, hanging back from the gathering of happy people greeting the arrivals in Cleveland. She is still pretty—that face that Grace would recognize through the cosmos—with her bobbed silver hair swept back from her face in a tortoiseshell headband, standing there in a pale pink cardigan, khakis, and cream-colored driving shoes. As the professor would say, *now there's a fine-looking woman.* No one would ever know that she is in the midst of crisis. Grace wants to take her narrow shoulders in her hands and shake her.

"Hi, honey," she says. Grace has to lean down a little and her mother hugs her with her elbows tucked in, not wanting to get too close. When she lets go, she holds her daughter at arm's length and says, "You're too thin, Grace. You need to eat more. There's leftover pork roast at home."

Grace rolls her suitcase and follows.

"How's Dad?"

"He opened his eyes today. And nodded his head. But they don't really know yet."

"How are you?"

"I'm fine," she says.

The view of Cleveland is brief. Smokestacks against the horizon. Terminal Tower, once indicative of a thriving industrial city. Despite its incessant efforts to revitalize, the city continues to crumble.

Grace somehow expected to see the bare, black tree trunks of winter, but as they drive east swiftly away from downtown, she is met with a Midwestern spring—the deciduous trees awash in pale green buds, daffodils crowding the bases of trees and signposts, the white bursts of apple blossoms. Even though she wishes it didn't, this place feels like home. The statuesque silhouettes of oaks. The gnarled branches of buckeyes and elms. She cracks her window for the smell, that mix of damp dirt and new grass and honeysuckle. She resents the beautiful veneer of where she grew up, its lie of tranquility. Nice and pristine on the surface, messy and angry underneath. Part of her would like to take a bulldozer right through the middle of every well-groomed lawn.

Her mother is quiet, and she drives with her gaze straight ahead. Grace knows she should reach out to the familiar thin-skinned hand that rests on her mother's lap and take it in her own. But she can't.

"George's went out of business," her mother says, as they pass a vacant shingled building where they used to go for birthdays and throw peanut shells on the floor. "No one went there anymore."

And that is the thing that makes Grace cry a little, silently, her face toward the side window. Callie loved that place.

"Kristen Mitchum is getting a divorce," her mother says. "She's going to move back in with Maureen and John. For the time being. I guess it's a good thing now that she couldn't get pregnant. He left her for his dentist."

Grace nods at the news of her childhood friend, the Mitchums a constant in her parents' narrative. She wonders what her mother could possibly tell them about her.

"Did he say anything yet?" Grace asks.

"Who?"

"Dad."

"Oh. Yes. A little. He's going to be just fine, Grace."

You don't know that, she wants to say.

They drive through the town of Hunter, Charles's hometown, past the polo field and the sweeping meadows, the horse barns and colonial mansions. Grace is already antsy to get back to New York.

"Mr. Chenowith has prostate cancer, but they caught it early," her mother says. "You'll have to go over and say hi to them sometime while you're home. Marjorie always asks about you."

The river is on the right, the Chagrin, rushing past, dark and swirling, its banks lined with sycamores and weeping willows, their thin hanging branches dipping into the water with the breeze. The car clicks into a lower gear as they climb the steep hill that turns into one of the few remaining nineteenth-century brick roads; a tunnel of overarching tree branches occludes the sky. And then they are on their street, Woodland Road, home to the Taylors, the Millers, the Mitchums, the Chenowiths, the Carlisles, the Coopers, and so on. No one ever leaves, and Grace feels the heavy tug of being pulled back in.

The driveway has been repaved recently, the fence at the entrance freshly painted white amidst the ivy. The juniper bushes are shaped and trimmed perfectly flat across their tops. The driveway curves around a cluster of pines, and as they approach the large house set on a bit of a hill, its side lawn gently rolling down, the first thing Grace thinks is that her parents must have felt giddy with adulthood and the rightness of their new life when they first bought it. Stone façade, white clapboard siding, black shutters. Built in 1836. A screened-in porch added in 1968. A flagstone walkway put in by her father in 1976. The front door is back to deep red after a brief period of forest green in the eighties. Near it, the crabapple tree her mother put in after Callie died is now giant and flush with pink petals.

"The house looks good, Mom," Grace says, slicing her finger scar with her thumbnail.

"Yes," her mother says, putting the car in park without pulling into the garage. "It's a good house. Maybe next time you won't feel the need to stay away for so long."

Her mother smiles and starts to get out, unable to say what she really wants to.

"I'm glad I came," Grace says.

"I am too. Though I suppose it wasn't exactly a choice, was it?"

Grace sits and watches as her mother shuts the car door, brushes a twig from the path with her toe, and then lets herself in through the side door by the kitchen.

Later, after her mother has retreated to bed, Grace tiptoes into her father's den. It smells the same, like leather and the must of old books, but it feels eerie. She feels like an impostor and, at the same time, a detective at a crime scene. His walnut rolltop desk is open and in disarray. Boxes of slide trays litter the floor. She falls into his big chair, molded so closely to his body, and rocks back with her feet against the ottoman. On the wall is a black-and-white picture of the four of them holding hands in a row, smiling in the sun, like a portal to a world that never existed. The house creaks and settles in the night wind. She can't relax. On the side table is a glass with the stale remains of whiskey. She drinks it like a shot and gags on its warm, medicinal thickness.

She forgoes the mahogany bar, always the centerpiece of the living room, and forages in the wine cellar off the basement. Unable to find the light, she grabs the nearest bottle, a Bordeaux from 1972, which would make her dad blanch. She takes it up to her bedroom with a mug she finds in the kitchen that says, "New York's the Big Apple but Cleveland's a Plum!"

Her room was redone after she left for college and she's thankful that it retains none of its girlhood ghosts. Like the rest of the house, it is spotless and ordered. Her mother now uses it for her study, a place to read—biographies mostly—and take care of Junior League business— she is chairwoman for the annual garden sale—and do crossword puzzles. The room is cloaked in red toile wallpaper. There's a rocking chair, a white iron daybed, and a cherry desk that used to hold sewing materials but now holds paper, envelopes, and the like. There are no photographs, there is no history.

Her mother has pulled the curtains and turned down the bed. Grace takes off her pants and, in underwear and a T-shirt, slides in, welcoming the clean coolness of the white, white sheets. The wine bottle balances on the thick beige carpeting below. She props up the pillows, pours the mug full, and situates a notebook on her knees.

Dear Charles,

I was so pleased to receive your letter. Thank you for responding and for the things you told me. I do understand about not being able to talk about the case. And certainly your need to be cautious is understandable. I'm sorry you have to use the inside of a pen but your writing is very neat and legible. Besides, it's not often that people write handwritten letters anymore.

As you can see from the return address, I have left Brooklyn to come home to my parents' house in Cuyahoga because my father has fallen ill.

You said you'd probably be willing to talk about your life, I would just need to ask. I guess I'd ask you to tell me about yourself from the beginning. My number here is below if you are allowed to use the phone. Please call.

She spills a crimson splotch on the comforter, and then turns it over to hide the stain.

#

The day is warming, but morning freshness lingers in the shade. Grace pulls on jeans and a sweater and a pair of her mother's bedroom slippers and pads out to the mailbox with her letter to Charles. She raises the red flag. She walks back to the house and around the side to her mother's tomato garden, a rectangle of dark new earth with two rows of vulnerable plants. The backyard is small and shaded by the edge of the woods that their neighborhood abuts. Grace steps gingerly over the logs and vines, trying to avoid the wet leaves and mud patches that have already seeped through the slipper soles, and sits on a fallen tree just far enough into the woods that she can't see any signs of civilization. She used to come out here when she was a kid and pretend she was lost in a forest. She would spin herself around and lie dizzily on the ground, looking up at the lattice of branches blocking the sky, and imagine that her family, the neighborhood, the world she knew had disappeared.

She looks up now, but it doesn't help shake the dread she feels about seeing her father. She can count on one hand the times that they have been alone together, each trying to avoid the strained conversation and silences, the blame for not being what the other needed.

When she was thirteen, during one of her parents' parties, Grace listened to her *Saturday Night Fever* record in her room while the glasses clinked below and she thought about Billy Cooper, who mowed their lawn in his jean jacket and Pink Floyd T-shirt. She had just reset the needle on "If I Can't Have You" for the third time when her door swung open. Mr. Morgenstern was a partner at the firm where her dad worked, a son of the founder, young, and as her mother used to say, *a bit of a playboy*. That night he was in jeans, which made Grace think he was cooler than the rest of the adults, and with his hand on the doorknob, he thrust his head into her room.

"Oh, hi," he said, acting surprised by her presence.

"Hi," she said, shyly.

He was handsome and she liked him. It was rumored that he smoked pot.

"I was looking for the bathroom," he said.

He ran his hand through his curly hair as he stepped into the room.

"Two down on the left," she said, turning down the volume of her record player.

"Hey, don't turn it down on my account. Can I hang out for a while? I'm a little bored with the old-timers downstairs."

She smiled, flattered, and said, "Okay."

He kicked the door closed behind him.

Instead of choosing the chair or even the bed, he sat down next to her on the floor, his leg touching hers. She inched away and he scooted closer. She laughed. She had long hair to her childish straight waist with barely an inkling of breasts, and she had done little more than kiss a boy over the summer as they wrestled one night in the sand trap of the tenth hole at the club.

Mr. Morgenstern pretended to study the foldout double-album case, nodding his head to the music.

"Did you like the movie?" he asked.

"Yeah," she said, even though she'd found it dark and strange. "I liked the dance scenes."

She smelled smoke and alcohol on him.

He set the album cover down and leaned his head back against the edge of her bed. He dropped his hand onto her knee. She laughed again because she thought it was a mistake, a joke of some kind. He looked at her, his eyes drunk and watery, and did not laugh back or even smile. He hand moved up her thigh and squeezed.

Grace froze, confused and scared.

"Mr. Morgenstern," she said.

"Hey, baby, call me Hank," he said, moving in to kiss her neck.

He pulled open the fly of his jeans and rolled over onto his knees, his hands now up her pink-striped Lacoste shirt. She tried to squirm away but knocked her head against the bedside table. She couldn't scream because she didn't want anyone to find them out; she knew it was somehow her fault.

There must have been a knock, but she didn't hear it.

"Grace?" Her dad stood in the doorframe.

Mr. Morgenstern was off her then. He jumped to his feet, hiking up his jeans in one swift motion.

"Hey, Jack," he said. "Must have gotten lost on the way to the bathroom."

With a cocky grin he pushed past her father.

"Grace?" her dad said quietly.

She started crying, pulling down her shirt, but she was so relieved. He would make it better.

"Are you okay?"

She nodded, and hugged her knees to her chest. More tears.

Her father could barely stand without swaying. He was loaded, of course.

"I'm sorry. God." He looked behind him and back at her. "The boss's son," he said, as if an excuse. "You're okay, sweetie, aren't you? You're not hurt or anything?"

His nose was red, his necktie loosened around his neck. He didn't go to her and she didn't run to him. He looked past her as she watched the carpeting. *Aren't you going to yell at him*, she thought, *aren't you on my side?* She remembers thinking that he would have done something if it had been Callie.

Her dad never said anything to Hank Morgenstern. Never mentioned it again. For all she knew, he didn't remember it the next day.

From then on she locked her bedroom door.

Her father's strange behavior in the weeks leading up to her return home was, the doctor said, the result of a small stroke, which often precedes a bigger one as it did in this case. It is unclear what damage has occurred. His speech is slow and slurred but he is able to respond to simple questions. They say his mind is fine, just trapped. His right side shows signs of paralysis but that seems to be improving by the hour, or so her mother tells her at the kitchen table when she goes back inside. Her mother has already been to the hospital and back.

"I wish you would have gotten me up," Grace says.

"That's not my job anymore, Grace," she says, pouring her some coffee. "You're a big girl."

"Were you trying to make a point by not waking me?"

"Grace," she says. "We'll go back this afternoon. He'll be glad to see you."

That she's not so sure about.

"I'm going out for a bit," her mother says. "I need to pick up your dad's shirts and get some more soil. Did you see the tomatoes I'm putting in?"

"I did. Impressive."

"I need to finish. And get the stakes in." She sponges away the brown dribble Grace's coffee cup has left on the table. "It's almost too late. It's been so warm."

Grace doesn't know when it happened but she feels like her mother has become someone to be careful with.

"Okay," Grace says. She wants her to sit. She wants her to stop. "Mom. Why don't you give me some things to do for you?"

"No, it's okay. I'd rather keep busy. You know this Saturday will be the first tee time your dad has missed in probably thirty years? We're lucky, you know. He's going to be okay."

"Sure he is," Grace says, feeling like some lame television character.

"So your job is good?" her mother asks, cleaning the coffee pot.

"No, Mom, I wouldn't say that. I don't think I've ever said that."

"Well, I just thought—"

"What?"

"I thought you liked your life in New York. I don't ever hear you complain about it."

Her mother dries her hands and slips back on her diamond ring.

"It's fine. Forget about it," Grace says.

"Maybe when you get married you won't have to work anymore."

"Sure, Mom. Keep up the positive thinking."

Her mother smoothes her hair and picks up her purse from the counter.

"I'll be back at two," she says. "And we'll go see your father."

## CHAPTER 12

Grace stands in the starkly lit hospital hall feeling woozy. Ever since the accident, when the three of them sat pie-eyed in the molded pea green plastic chairs, waiting for the official pronouncement that they already knew, hospitals have made her feel faint. After a minute, her mother motions for her to enter the room.

He is propped up in bed, his once-blond hair now white, thinning in front and sticking up in back against the pillow. His face has uncharacteristic sallowness and sag, making the broken blood vessels of his nose more prominent. He looks small in the faded gown tied around his neck like a baby bib, the fabric worn around the collar from innumerable washings in boiling institutional machines. A pulse monitor is clamped to his index finger and he is connected to an IV.

"Hi, Dad," she says, approaching the bed, trying to sound peppy.

He looks from his wife to his daughter. His eyes go blank and then narrow in what looks like anger. He grunts.

"Nice to see you," Grace says.

"Jack," her mother says, "Grace is home for a visit."

The nurse says quietly, "It's natural for stroke patients to be angry and frustrated. Sometimes they can be aggressive. Don't take it personal. He's just acting out a bit."

Grace stands woodenly and, not knowing what to do with her hands, buries them in her pockets.

"Don't let him fool you," the nurse says, marking something on his chart. "He'll behave and be ready to go home in no time." She winks.

"Thanks," her mother says, allowing the woman a chilly smile.

Her father says something indecipherable. He says it again and Grace hears him say "bitch" while looking at her.

"What's that?" her mom asks, patting his hand.

"I know about you," he says with immense angry effort, lifting his arm in Grace's direction. Breathing heavily his head lolls toward the window.

She shrinks smaller and smaller.

*   *   *

Hunter is one town over, similar to Cuyahoga but wealthier and more exclusive. The Raggatts live on Lily Pond Lane, an immaculate street with a large pond at its end, home to big new money, including a rumored mafia family, a grocery store magnate, and a part-owner of the Cavaliers. The ladies at the club would say *it's a tad gauche*. Grace takes her mother's car and, encased in its chestnut leather interior, drives into the enclave.

She slows to look at each massive house, wondering which is theirs, ruling out homes here and there, one with a swing set, one with an elderly woman pruning roses, one with a marble fountain in the driveway. The pitched roof of an imposing Tudor rises up above a privet hedge and there is something about the perfectly clean edge of the lawn and sad dark windows that makes her think, *maybe*. There's nowhere to park without looking conspicuous on this street, even in her mother's Mercedes, so she idles, looking at the house for any signs before slowly turning around in the cul-de-sac. As she rolls back out, an incoming silver SUV with a well-kept blond behind the wheel passes. Grace's heart quickens. It's her. *Nice to meet you, Mrs. Raggatt*. She looks a lot like she did as Miss Ohio, a well-preserved older version. Grace watches in her rearview as the car turns up the driveway. She imagines Charles behind one of the upstairs windows, dreaming of what freedom could mean.

It's getting late but Grace doesn't want to go home. She drives toward the city and turns on Prospect, the street where she and Callie would joyously point out hookers from the windows of the station wagon as they drove to the airport. They were wild-haired women in spandex hot pants, their hands balled up in the pockets of short, rabbit-fur jackets, teetering on four-inch Lucite platform heels, even in winter, even on a Sunday morning. The women would laugh and do little dances, their listless stares lifted for just a moment.

"Don't look at them, girls," her mother would say.

But Grace knew her dad was looking, too, at the dark equine thighs and unfettered breasts.

There are fewer transient hotels now, and no streetwalkers in the twilight glow. She finds a worn-down place with neon beer signs, wooden booths, and plastic bowls of stale yellow popcorn. Although she is the only white person and the only woman, the crowd, mainly middle-aged men, doesn't seem to care. In her oversized sweater and saggy dirty jeans, she doesn't arouse much interest.

Grace orders two ginger ales from the bartender, a small white-haired man who smiles a little but doesn't say anything. She drinks one down and hands him back the glass, taking the other one with her to a table.

"Popcorn?" he says to her back.

A guy at the bar laughs.

"No thanks," she says over her shoulder.

She sits and thinks of Charles and how it feels for him, for them, to have always known that they could never be the golden people. Like Sarah Shafer. Like Callie.

"You're like Pigpen," her father once teased, "but instead of dirt, you have a black cloud following you around." He had laughed then, and kissed the top of her head.

What if Charles, in some way, had simply let it happen? If he knew something but did nothing and then she was dead. And maybe the guilt he felt for his inaction made him confess to what he didn't do. *It's possible*, she thinks.

A man sits down across from Grace and rests his chin on his clasped hands. He is younger than the others in the bar, with a look that is both lascivious and contemptuous.

"What's up?" he says.

"Nothing," she says.

"Come here often?" he asks.

Men snicker in the background. Despite his slight smile, the man's eyes are hard and never waver from her. His forearms are well defined and scarred.

"No. First time," she says.

"Took a wrong turn on the way to the 'burbs?"

She looks up and the men at the bar are looking at her, waiting for her reaction, waiting for her recognition that she is not wanted here.

"Okay," she says. "I'm going to go."

"Now hold up. You haven't told us your name yet."

The man sucks his teeth and licks his lips. Grace stands and he reaches out to graze her arm with the back of his fingers.

"Too bad," he says. "You know I was just playing with you." He waves his fingers and says, "You go on now."

She hears whistles and laughter behind her as she pushes through the door out into the chilly night, feeling as out of place as the ridiculous Mercedes that hugs the curb, alone in the dull flickering bulb of the streetlight.

She locks the doors quickly after she gets behind the wheel, and then stares at the haze of city lights. She starts the car, and once she gets going, opens the window to keep cold air on her face.

By the time she pulls into the driveway, her hands hurt from grasping the wheel. She has clearly missed dinner; her mother would have had it ready at seven. Her parents' bedroom is dark but her mother has left the kitchen light on.

Grace finds her dinner plate wrapped in cellophane in the refrigerator. She carries it with her to her father's den and collapses into his chair, eating a cold string bean with her fingers.

I know about you.

She has always assumed that no one saw the accident. No one ever said anything to the contrary. Here in his chair, only the trees are visible through the front window. But what if he wasn't in his chair? She stands up, and the view of the lawn opens up. What if he was at the window, looking out at them playing in the front yard, watching

Callic run, her braids bouncing, watching Grace get angry at her for opening her eyes while she was It, for cheating, for thinking she could always get away with everything?

# # #

Grace wakes up in the gray light to the insistent call of turtledoves. She is cold and curled up in the chair, a throbbing ache between her eyes, cuddling an overturned plate of congealed chicken marsala.

## CHAPTER 13

Caroline *is fourteen and athletic and cute. She doesn't try to be liked. She just is. And she's also comfortable enough with herself to be earnest and cool at the same time. She is your sister and, by far, your favorite person. She is a freshman and you are a senior. When you see her in school, she always gives you a hug, regardless of who's around. You like it even when you'd rather she didn't. Despite your envy of the way life lets her cruise along, you love sweet Caroline because she is perhaps the only one in the world who doesn't think you're a loser.*

You start up the stairs, two at a time, but midway you slow to a walk, your sneakers leaving bearlike prints in the wheat-colored carpeting. Caroline's door is closed. You knock with the same code—the beginning of Bewitched— *that you two have used since you were small, and you push the door open.*

*"You're supposed to wait until I say it's okay to come in,"
she says. "What if I was naked or something?"*

*"Like I would give a shit," you say and jump beside her
onto her big, pink-duveted bed.*

*She holds her pet lop-eared rabbit on her stomach. Its
deep brown bunny eyes twitch. You don't like how vulnerable it is. It makes you nervous.*

"Buns has a brain the size of a pea," you say.

"Shut up! I know she's super-smart," she says.

Your mother calls you for dinner.

*Charles Sr. is already at the table, sipping his Glenlivet,
scanning the* Wall Street Journal. *He is gray-templed and fit,
and his reading glasses are parked halfway down his nose.*

"Hi, kids," he says. "How was school today?"

He turns back to the paper before either of you answer.

*"Fine, Dad," Caroline says in a phony chipper voice,
making googly eyes at you.*

*You know your father doesn't think that highly of you,
that he is confused by your lack of friends, by your inepti-
tude in sports, by your refusal to fit in. He was thrilled when
it became clear that Caroline was normal and liked what
other girls liked and didn't spend hours alone, locked in her
room, trying to fuse the different parts of herself together.*

*"Sweetheart," your mom says, "it's dinner. Enough of
your paper."*

He dutifully folds it and tosses it back onto the counter.

"What will you be doing in Denver?" she asks him.

He says, chewing, "Uh, looking to close some financing with a group out there."

You have no idea what your dad does. You're pretty sure your mom and Caroline don't know either.

Aside from forks and knives against plates, it is quiet. You want to ask him if he is really your father. You have the same nose and the same shaped face so there's probably a biological connection, but he is so far from understanding anything about you it's comical. You wonder if he wishes you would become someone else or if he would rather you just go away.

Caroline kicks you under the table.

"I read this article that said that the French make their appliances in the spirit of telephones and Americans make theirs in the spirit of cars. Isn't that so true?" your mother asks.

"I don't get it," Charles Sr. says.

"Mom," Caroline says, "I'm going over to Jen's tomorrow night after field hockey."

You never have anywhere to go.

Your mother cuts a prawn into tiny pieces but lets them sit in the buttery sauce on the plate. Both of your parents lob comments into the space above the table, hoping someone will come to the rescue and scoop the words up, to keep the conversation afloat. They pretend that they are talking because if they drop the ruse, they will have to admit their discontent. For having enough money. For always wanting more. For not being soothed by new cars and fresh flowers and filet mignon. For not being able to keep the deer from munching on newly transplanted shrubs. For eventually keeping them all away.

After dinner, you quickly eat a pint of Ben & Jerry's Half Baked while Caroline disappears to talk on the phone. You slink to the cocoon of your room, slip off your shoes, and fall back on the bed, exhaling fiercely. It's worse at night sometimes, the feeling that things might never change. You press the heels of your palms against your eyelids to keep the thoughts away.

# # #

You've had a crush on Hadley Jameson for years, ever since she sat next to you on the bus in fifth grade on a field trip to the symphony. Her hair is longer now but still caramel-streaked and, you imagine, as soft as the underbelly of your sister's rabbit. Hadley always smiles at you in the halls and she says your name when she talks to you. Despite her kindness to you, she is extremely popular. She is followed by chatty girls and pursued by muscular boys. Her skin is allover dewy like she just came back from a chilly morning jog. Her small breasts press firmly against the navy blue and orange stripes of her cheerleading sweater.

You gave her a ride home last week and she touched your thick forearm when she said goodbye. Maybe, you think.

Mr. Phelps talks about sunk costs and you are glad to be in the back row so you can ponder Hadley. In your daydream she is herself but you are thirty pounds lighter and clear-skinned with sun-touched cheeks. You are at ease.

"Hey, Raggatt."

Randy is a soccer player with a lean torso and slightly bowed legs. When he sweats during practice, his black hair curls up around his face like a servant boy in your mom's Caravaggio coffee-table book. He kicks your chair.

"Hey, Raggatt."

"Yeah?"

"So what's up, man?"

"Nothing much."

"We're thinking about getting together tonight after practice. Drinking some brewskies."

"That sounds good," you say, knowing what is following before you can put a stop to the words. "I could pitch in some, if you want."

"Yeah. Okay. That would be cool. Give me like twenty bucks. That should do it. I'll let you know where we're meeting up."

"Okay," you say, thinking that maybe this one time you will have things to say to make the guys laugh and slap you on the back.

You pull out your wallet and hand some crumpled bills behind you. It may have been forty instead of twenty. It doesn't matter.

"Thanks, man. I'll catch you later," he says.

You wish you had lips like his, dark and full and wanted.

You are the one with the money. It is your only way in. It's no secret and you don't fool yourself. Hey, you think, at least you have that. What if you were you and you were poor on top of it? That gives you something to like about Charles Raggatt Sr., CEO, Remsfield Capital.

When the bell rings, you go where you always go for lunch: upstairs to the drama room. Sometimes Ms. Burnes is up there and sometimes she isn't, but she always lets you and Steve hang out within her domain. You don't want to like Steve, he's effeminate and his idea of fun is renting Okla-homa *or going to* The Rocky Horror Picture Show, *but you tolerate him because he tolerates you. He would say you guys are friends, and that is something in itself. Sometimes Kelly comes by when her goth friends have cut school and she has nowhere else to go. She pierced her own nose last weekend and now it's swollen and crusty so you aren't surprised to see her, slumped in a corner beanbag chair, coloring her finger-nails black with a marker.*

"How come you're so happy, preppy? Did you get an-other car or something?"

Kelly's nose is disgusting. One nostril is twice the size of the other and there is a greenish discharge where the ring cuts through the skin. You must wrinkle your face in distaste because she laughs and touches it lightly with her forefinger.

"Hello to you, too," you say, tacking up a corner of a Renaissance Fair poster that has slipped from the bulletin board.

Steve throws a piece of celery stick at Kelly. His bangs hang low across his face so he constantly flicks his head to shake them from his eyes. He pretends he likes girls but you know he doesn't.

You sit on the floor between them, take out your lunch from your backpack, and start in on a large bag of Doritos. Kelly reaches quickly for a handful, leaving a trail of bright orange cheese dust on her shelflike chest. She is, as usual, in head-to-toe black—leggings, skirt over the leggings, T-shirt, big-soled shoes. She redraws a fake rose tattoo on her ankle with colored markers every day. You know she's not so tough or she would have a real one already. She pops her headphones on, the music audibly tinny and angry.

"Are you going to the dance on Friday?" you ask Steve.

"Are you kidding?"

"It could be fun," you say.

Hadley will be there. It will be dark and romantic and you will look good and Hadley will be there.

"I'd rather eat glass," Steve says, flipping his hair.

"I don't know," you say.

Steve blinks. "What are you talking about?"

You reach for a pack of slightly crushed Ding Dongs. "Whatever," he says, visibly miffed but not altogether dismissive, and for that you are grateful.

He crosses his arms and whistles a tune you don't recognize, staring up at the miniature model of the Old Globe Theatre next to Ms. Burnes's desk. Steve is always on a diet and he has already finished his small bag of celery and carrot sticks. You tilt the bag of Doritos in his direction and he takes one daintily between two fingers.

"Just forget it," you say.

You have to pull your pants up a bit under your gut when you get to your feet. Kelly's eyes are closed but she gives you the finger as you leave.

You are sitting in the front seat of your car, a BMW, blue, just two months old. It's September but still hot and humid. You're parked in the lot behind the Home Depot, your air conditioner on high.

You wipe your palms on your chinos and breathe through your nose. There is a humming sound just beyond your perception that gnaws at the edge of your concentration. You believe it and you don't believe it. That someone could like you, that Hadley Jameson could like you.

"I liked the cheer you guys did at assembly last week. It was really cool how you got flipped in the air," you imagine yourself saying to her. You squeeze your eyes closed as hard as you can to keep in focus, to not lose the thread. You feel as though it is starting to loosen from the spool and fall in soft loops.

You drive to the 7-Eleven near school again, hoping to run into Randy or one of his cohorts. It's already five and no one has told you where to meet for the party.

You hold a cup under the cola Slurpee spout and watch

the ice froth billow out in soft mounds. You drink it down fast, welcoming the cold headache that blots out all thoughts. You pretend you're looking for something between the Blistex and the shoelaces because the pimply kid behind the counter saw you in here earlier and watches you a little too closely, like you are about to stuff a corn dog into your pocket and flee. A muted ding-ding signals the front door opening behind you, but you don't want to turn too quickly and expose your eagerness or your reason for browsing, for the third time today, in the 7-Eleven.

Randy jerks his head a bit in greeting like the other soccer and football players do as he glides in from outside. Once, after a round of practicing in the bathroom mirror, you tried doing this head flick to Steve, but he laughed so fast the coffee yogurt he was eating came up through his nose.

"Hey, bro," you say, with a quick glance Randy's way before going back to gazing intensely at a bottle of WD-40. He goes straight for the Gatorade. "So, uh...What's up?"

"Just got out of practice."

Randy drinks half the bottle before reaching the counter. His legs glisten with post-scrimmage sweat, an outline where his shin guards were.

You wait, scraping the skin around your thumbs with the nails of your forefingers. You wait, even while Randy rips open the Velcro of his wallet. You wait as he fishes a couple of ones from the billfold.

"*Hey,*" *you say, hoping you sound laid-back, even though you fear you sound pinched and whiney. He doesn't respond as he drains the rest of the yellow-green liquid. "So, Randy.*"

You can feel the heat of his skin through his jersey before your hand reaches his shoulder.

"*Huh?*"

You want to ask him where the party is, why you keep paying for beer for gatherings where you're not wanted, why you aren't—and won't ever be—one of them, why it's so hard to keep trying from day to day and not be any closer to what you think it is you want.

"*Dude?*" *Randy asks, clearly impatient to make his exit. He stands in the open doorway.*

You run your hand over your hair, gelled to a crisp.

"*Nothing,*" *you say. "I guess I'll see you around.*"

"*Later,*" *he says, as he launches the empty Gatorade bottle into the trash.*

Once outside, it takes a minute for you to notice. You don't see anything until you're in the car and look in your rearview to pull out. Something on your back window. White and foamy. Letters. Words. You walk around you car.

RAGGATT

=

FAGGOT

The shaving cream has started to melt and the letters are running together, but they may as well be carved into you. You look around. You fake a laugh in case anyone is watching. Your face is hot and swirling. You swipe your sleeve across the window and shake your arm off onto the parking lot. You get in the car. There is shaving cream in your hair.

To get home you drive north along the western edge of town and the sixteenth hole of Hunter Country Club's golf course. Breathe. Ignore it. Pretend it's all a joke. The shorn, deep green of the course is opulent in the dusk light. You turn onto Lily Pond Lane, where the large houses are set back from the road by huge lawns and clusters of oaks and maples and evergreen hedges.

Do not think about it, do not see those words.

As you pull up your sloped driveway, the late afternoon sun is setting and the colors of the yard are saturated. You sit in the car a long time, watching the light change around you.

Inside the house you go upstairs hoping to find Caroline, but no one is home. In the corner of the room, you see the bunny's eyes reflect the light.

Fucking soft fur and innocence. You are flooded with shame and despair and fury. Make it stop. Make it better. Something slips, too deep to ever reach and put back in place.

You jerk the animal out of the cage by its ears as it shimmies and works its legs in a frenzy. It makes a slight mewing sound like a cat, which makes you even angrier. You stun it by whacking it hard against the wall in the hallway. You like the power of the pulsing life and small bones in your hand. You like the feral smell of fear. The rabbit pees on the kitchen floor before you make it outside.

From the pile of bricks for your mom's garden pathway, you take a jagged chunk in your free hand. Your body feels taught and electric and with one swift bash, you crush the rabbit's skull between brick and dirt. Stop. Just stop. It spins its leg for a while and then is still. You pound its head again and again until all that remains is torn and bloody fur.

It is quiet and cool amidst the pine trees. You throw the piece of brick as far as you can and kick the carcass down the embankment and into a pile of leaves and moss. You feel better. You feel calm. For the briefest of moments. Until you feel awful, cold to your toes, inhuman. You will never tell Caroline.

You push it down and down and down.

The Emeryville College student charged in the murder of a classmate is under suicide watch in a jail psychiatric ward today as his lawyer said he was busy preparing a psychiatric defense. The lawyer, Robert Dubno, said that he would pursue a defense that Charles Raggatt, 19, "is certainly not legally responsible for his acts."

## CHAPTER 14

Over the past few days, Grace's father's motor skills have improved, and he has come home from the hospital. In the mornings he seems more like himself, even though it's still an effort to get words out. By midday, his frustration at his body usually leads to sullen withdrawal. He spills his tomato juice down his chin. He takes the stairs slowly, one foot and then the other, leaning heavily on the banister, refusing help to get up to the bedroom. Grace found him standing at his bar last night, trying to get the top off a bottle, which she takes as a sign that he is becoming his old self again.

Today her mother has taken him to physical therapy so Grace drinks her coffee and walks through the empty house, infiltrated by the muted sounds of a lawnmower, birds, and hammering from the Coopers' new construction. She leaves a message for Brian that she will need more time off and she hopes it's okay and the number here if he needs to reach her, knowing of course that he won't. She sits on the carpet against a newly re-covered couch in the rarely used living room and warms her feet in the sun. Charles has received her letter by now. Her head feels wooly. It's the third day she hasn't had a drink.

She remembers the empty bottle of Bordeaux she has in her room from the first night, currently under the bed, which her mother will discover soon if she doesn't sneak it out.

The phone rings and her heart skids, but it's only the dentist's office with an appointment reminder for her dad.

"I think he has to cancel," Grace says.

With the bottle in her fist, she walks out to the curb in her slippers and robe and nestles it discreetly beneath a bulging bag of grass clippings. Three different lawn crews are parked along the street, cutting, trimming, mulching, and watering almost every house in the neighborhood. At the mailbox she sifts through the garden and golf catalogs, investment statements and credit card bills, searching for that telltale handwriting. Nothing.

The phone rings again.

"I've got it!" she yells, running back up the driveway, even though no one is home.

She bursts through the door and knocks the phone off its cradle.

"Hello?" she says, panting. "Hello?"

"This is a recording. You have a collect call from an inmate of the Nassau County jail. Will you accept the charges?"

"Yes! Of course, yes."

There is a whirring sound and then a click.

"Hello?" she says.

"Hello. Hi. Is this Grace?"

"Yes," she says, trying not to blurt everything out at once.

"Um, hello," he says slowly. "This is Charles. Charles Raggatt. Thank you for your letter." His delivery is halting and formal, yet underneath he sounds young, not yet a man.

She slides her back along the wall, down to the floor.

"You're welcome. Hi. How are you?"

"Oh," he says. There is an angry exchange in the background. "Well, I'm okay. How about you?"

"I'm pretty good," she says, smiling. "Thanks for calling."

There is a pause on the other end.

"So I don't know what you want to know about me. I'm not really used to talking about myself."

"I want to hear anything," she says. "Anything you feel like sharing."

"There's this quote I have. It's one of my favorites. I thought I could read it to you. Do you want to hear it?"

"Sure. Yes."

"It goes, 'I have striven not to laugh at human actions, not to weep at them, not to hate them, but to understand them.'"

"Who said that?" she asks.

"Someone named Spinoza."

"He was a philosopher, right?"

"I don't know. I copied it from a book. I have a book of famous quotations that I like to flip through."

"It's a good one," she says.

He doesn't respond.

"Charles?"

"I don't know what to say," he says.

"Tell me about your life. I want to try and understand."

"It's not that interesting."

"It is to me. I don't believe what I read." She squeezes her hand into a fist, waiting out his pause. "Maybe you can tell me about your family."

"Okay. I guess I can do that," he says. "My parents are Kathy, well Katherine, and Charles Raggatt Sr., who I'm named after. People think my mom is pretty nice. Decorating the house is real important to her. She's kind of a nervous person. She's always looking around at what other people are doing. She's tense even when she tries to seem relaxed. I mean, even when it looks like she's relaxing she never is. She was a beauty queen after high school. She showed me her Miss Ohio sash once. It's white satin with cursive blue writing. She keeps it folded up in her jewelry box. She likes to say that she didn't win Miss America but she won a husband, because a friend introduced her to my dad the night of the pageant."

Charles stops talking. Grace presses her ear into the phone. Someone yells, "Hurry it up, yo!"

"What about your dad?" she asks.

"My dad. Well, um…He's successful in business. He makes a lot of money. He really likes the Indians. His company has a loge at the stadium every season. When I was young I went with him a few times. I liked the snacks and the big chairs. But I didn't care about the games so he stopped taking me. He bought me a rowing machine a couple years ago. It just showed up in my room. I guess he wanted me to lose weight. But I never used it."

"Did you get along with you parents?"

He pauses and sniffles.

"I got along with them okay, I guess. It's not like we had big fights or anything. My mom didn't like that I was, I don't know, different from other kids. She tried to pretend it was going better for me than it was and that it would get better if I tried harder to fit in. My dad gave up on me pretty early on," he says softly. "I preferred to be by myself. And, I don't know. He wasn't mean or anything. We just kind of did our own thing. One time I was having a hard time and I tried to tell him. They never knew how it was."

Charles sounds listless and monotone.

"Have you seen them since…"

"Did you know I didn't talk until much later than other kids?" he asks.

"No, I didn't know that," she says, smiling to herself.

"It's not like I couldn't. I mean, I knew how to talk and sometimes when I was alone, I would talk to myself."

He is quiet.

"I know it wasn't how they are saying," she says.

"I can't talk about that."

"That's okay."

"I heard someone say one time that people have kids to find themselves. I don't think my parents liked what they found."

There is commotion on the other end.

"Charles?"

"But I don't blame them for how I turned out or any-thing."

"Okay," she says.

"It's confusing here sometimes. And loud. I'm sorry if I ramble."

"No, you're fine. Don't worry about it."

Grace strains against his long delay, trying not to jump in and fill the silence.

"So you're in Ohio?" he asks, momentarily brightened.

"Yeah, for a little while."

"I haven't been back there in a long time."

"It's spring. The dogwoods are in bloom."

"I'm allowed to go out a little bit but I don't. I get two and a half minutes in the shower and I go when everyone else is outside. It's not like I don't have plenty to think about." His voice catches.

"You have a sister, right?" Grace asks.

"I have a little sister. Sweet Caroline, like the song. We get along great. She's a sophomore in high school. Everybody likes her."

"Do you two talk?"

"I got a letter from her at the beginning but I haven't heard from her in a while. It's a great letter though. She got a new kitten." His voice trails off.

"Charles?"

"I have to go now."

"You'll call again?"

"Goodbye, Grace."

"Charles," she says, but the phone is dead.

⚓ ⚓ ⚓

Grace tracks down Hadley Jameson, Charles's crush from high school, at Ohio State, who sounds genuinely saddened about him and willing to talk about the boy she remembers. Grace drives to Columbus and meets her in front of the McDonald's in the student union, amidst a throng of kids and fast-food smells. Hadley is the embodiment of perky. Thick, sandy-colored hair pulled back in a bouncy high ponytail, small nose, dimples. She is sporty and girlish in a short denim skirt and it's easy to imagine her at home in a cheerleading uniform. As she sits, she mouths, "Hi!" with exaggerated excitement to someone who passes behind Grace, and then turns back with rapt attention.

"It is *so* disturbing," Hadley says, making her blue eyes big. "My friend Rebecca called me from UVA—her mom had told her—and I totally couldn't believe it. Not Charles. Well really, not anybody, but Charles? He seemed like such a child in a way. Innocent or something."

"Were you friends?" Grace asks, curious as to what she'll say.

"Kind of. I mean we were friendly. He gave me rides home sometimes. I've known him since the fifth grade. We met on the bus going to Severance Hall. You're from Cleveland, right?"

"Cuyahoga. I'm home visiting my parents."

"Oh, that's awesome. I love being home. I still get way homesick. I'm going back to Hunter for the summer. To be a lifeguard."

"Was Charles picked on a lot in school?" Grace asks.

"I don't think so. Not that I know of. I don't know what high school was like when you were young, but it really was pretty unified at Hunter."

Grace passed through four years of high school in a fog of detachment, smoking pot alone in her room, blowing smoke out the window and spraying Love's Baby Soft to cover it up. She had some casual friends, but she never revealed much. Surface was easy. Especially when everyone else was looking for someone to listen.

"But there were cliques, right?" Grace asks. "Some kids who were outcasts?"

"I don't know. People were nice to each other. There weren't, like, bullies or anything."

"I thought there was some incident with a note," Grace says.

"Oh. You heard about that? That was a prank that got out of hand. I guess those guys can kind of be jerks. I didn't know about it until after. I felt bad about it but Charles said it was no big deal."

Hadley's face has lost a bit of its life. She bites her lip.

"I assume it wasn't a big secret that he liked you?" Grace asks.

"Yeah, I knew he liked me, but what was I supposed to do? Stop talking to him? Tell him I wasn't interested?" Hadley says, with a trace of impatience. She pauses and regroups. "Have you heard about the party he had senior year? His parents threw this over-the-top bash for graduation and invited everybody. They must have spent thousands of dollars on it. There were tables of food everywhere. Caterers running around. A DJ and a dance floor put in on the lawn. Carnival games. The whole thing was so weird and kind of mortifying, especially because it was for Charles. His parents were there greeting people— it looked like they were hired actors, smiling and pretending that their son was popular. The football players were plastered, knocking things over and laughing. No one even talked to Charles. I found him up in his room. That was the last time I saw him. He was really excited about leaving for college, that whole 'I can't wait to get out of this town' thing. He seemed really psyched."

Grace imagines his unwavering belief that he could start over as someone new.

"I loved high school," Hadley says. "But I know it isn't as fun for some people. It's sad, you know?"

#

By the time Grace arrives home, the day has dipped past dusk and the afterglow of the sun hangs pinkish behind the woods, deepening to blood orange down near the horizon. The house is all lit up.

"Nice of you to join us, Grace," her mother says, already seated in the dining room.

It is the first time in years that the three of them are sitting down to dinner. Her father is in his head-of-the-table spot, still commanding despite his frailty. He has dressed for the occasion in a French blue oxford shirt, and Grace wonders if he fastened the buttons himself.

"Sorry I'm late," she says. "There was some traffic."

Her father lifts his drink shakily to his lips and her mother adjusts the napkin in her lap.

"Looking good, Dad," Grace says.

He smiles and winks at her and there he is, the old

charmer whose fickle attentions she has always coveted. His speech is thick and strained.

"Thanks, sweetie," he says.

She hasn't heard this from him since she was a child.

The plate in front of her is filled with steak, mashed potatoes, and green beans. There is a wineglass set at her place but she doesn't fill it. She will go another day. She thinks about Charles, adrift in high school. She wonders what he thinks about for all the hours.

"A celebration dinner," her mother says. She has lipstick on, and her pearls. "We had a good day today. The therapist says it'll take some work, but your dad will be as good as new. Back to normal."

"That's great," Grace says, her enthusiasm forced.

Her father picks up his knife and fork and fights to separate a piece of steak. His frustration mounts and his utensils clang against his plate. Her mother nudges her under the table and Grace looks away, taking a bite of potatoes.

He gets a piece of meat free. They eat for a while in silence.

"So, Grace. Are you seeing anyone special these days?" her mother asks.

"No," she says. "I was for a while. A literature professor from City College. But we broke up."

Her father chews and stares at her without comment.

"Oh. I'm sorry," her mother says. "It seems much

more difficult nowadays. But you'll find someone."

"It's okay. It's not my goal in life. I'm not waiting to be completed," Grace says.

It falls quiet again.

"What were you up to today in Columbus?" her mother asks.

"I have a project I'm working on."

"For the magazine?"

"No. On my own."

"What kind of project?" she asks.

"I'm investigating a murder."

"What? What do you mean?" her mother asks, cocking her head to mask her pained expression.

Her father makes an odd, high-pitched sound like a wheeze and starts coughing.

"Jack!"

"Fine," he says putting his hand up, regaining his breath. "I'm fine."

"Because I don't believe the story about him," Grace says.

"The murderer?"

"Yes. The kid being charged."

"Oh, Grace," her mother says, looking past her out the window. "Why waste your time on someone like that? What are you doing?"

"I don't think it's a waste of time," Grace says. "To help someone."

"To help someone?"

"To try. To pursue the truth."

Grace stares at her mother, defiant, even as she fears she is chasing dizzily after something she may never know.

"I don't understand this, Grace."

"I talked to him today. The kid who's accused. So don't be alarmed if you see collect calls from a New York jail on your phone bill."

It's the end of the uneasy peace. Her father spills his water reaching for his bourbon, then can't make his hand work well enough to right the glass.

"Jack, let me help you," her mother says.

"Susan, please," he says. "I've got it."

He sets the glass upright but there is a puddle of water on his plate. He looks at it and then at them.

"Goddamnit all," he says and pushes away from the table.

He muddles off to the bar, then withdraws to the haven of his den.

Her mother stares at the center of the table.

"More wine, Mom?" Grace asks, picking up the bottle.

"No, thank you," she says.

So Grace fills her own glass to the rim and drinks it down before she can change her mind. It tastes so good, the familiar promise of solace. She fills her glass again.

"I'm worried about you," her mother says.

"Don't be."

Her mother scrapes the remnants of the plates onto hers but doesn't get up. She rolls the wine around her glass and takes a sip.

"Mom."

"Hmm?"

"Why did you put up with him?"

Grace looks steadily at her mother, who twists her necklace around her forefinger.

"I don't think this is an appropriate conversation," she says.

"I want to know," Grace says. "Tell me."

"Keep your voice down," her mother says.

But Grace can see the smallest hint of an opening in her tired eyes.

Her mother stacks the plates and stands.

"Mom. Leave it. I'll do it."

"No, it's fine. I'll do it," she says.

"I'll do it!" Grace says, yanking the plates from her. "You don't always have to do everything. I'll clean up."

And for the first time ever, her mother lets her. She sits back down and works the cork back into the bottle.

"Marriage involves a lot of putting up with," her mother says. "That's the commitment."

When dissatisfaction turns to antipathy and then to apathy, Grace thinks.

"Sounds like fun."

"It's not like he hasn't put up with things, too. Who among us is perfect?"

"Not you?" Grace says.

Her mother smiles a little but doesn't divulge further. She folds her napkin. Grace rises from her chair.

"I thought he might leave me once," her mother says quietly.

"What?" Grace sets the plates on the table and waits.

"When I was pregnant with Callie. I suspected he was having an affair with one of the secretaries in his office. Janice."

"I remember her. The flaming red hair."

Her mother nods.

"But when Callie was born, something changed. I don't know what it was. She was a good omen. And he came back to us with renewed purpose." She looks down at her lap and then back up. "And I was always thankful that he did."

"And that was enough for you?"

"Where there's an ebb, there will always be a flow, Grace." Her mother stands and walks towards the living room. "There's always a reason to be optimistic."

Grace runs the water in the sink to get it hot. Her mother is a neat cook, cleaning up as she goes, so there is little to do but wash a pan and load the dishwasher. But Grace wants to make a mess. She takes one of the plates and drops it on the floor, the shards splitting like a sunburst.

"Grace?"

"It's all okay," she calls back with mocking cheer.

She sweeps up the dirty pieces. *Of course it was Callie who brought him back*, she thinks.

Grace takes the wine bottle outside, kicking off her shoes on the front steps. The grass is cold and soft, lit by the slice of moon overhead. She walks across the front lawn, down its subtle grade, and turns around, looking back at the house. A light is on in her dad's den on the far right, and in the upper left, in her parents' bedroom. She leans against the trunk of one of the low-branched sugar maples she and Callie used to climb, and rubs her hand against the bark. She places the bottle in a crook of the tree, then hoists herself up, her foot in the V-shaped crutch where the trunk splits in two, just as she remembers it, the perfect step. She shimmies up to a new level, reaching down for the bottle. The bark and knots gouge her feet, but she is surprised by her nimble handling. The lone streetlamp is close enough to light her way. Up and up. She can no longer see the ground in the dark but she doesn't care. She will not think about what comes next or how to get back down. She settles on a limb and uncorks.

The Taylors' husky has gotten out and trots down the street, looking around, catching Grace's scent perhaps, but not considering that she might be in the tree above. Somewhere in the distance the faint roar of a motorcycle engine rises and then fades out.

When Grace finishes the last swallow, she hurls the empty bottle as far as her spindly arm can throw, sending glass splintering and skidding across Woodland Road, crashing through the suburban quiet. And then there are only the night sounds of crickets and leaves, once again.

## CHAPTER 15

When Grace awakes at dawn, shivering, it is to the pat-pat-pat of the jogging feet of tiny, white-haired Mrs. Taylor, anorexic for thirty years, known to push the food around her plate at every dinner party and run for an hour every morning, her shoulder bones sharp through her windbreaker. Grace shifts her sore neck to watch. The bottle glass crunches under Mrs. Taylor's small feet. She looks down and around but doesn't stop.

In the growing light of the morning, Grace begins to realize that she is stuck in this aerie of new green leaves. The branches sway and squeak against each other when the wind blows. She can't feel her feet and her hands are scraped and red from the cold. She manages to slide down a level but she's still up high and afraid she might fall and break her neck. She's stranded like a cat, ashamed by her predicament.

Below, her father appears, an apparition out of the mist, shuffling from the garage in his navy mono-grammed pajamas and leather slippers, still having trouble getting his legs to work how he wants them to. He has a golf club in his hand. A driver. Of course, Saturday morning tee time. Grace's shoulders hunch in sadness. He has always been impeccably groomed, no matter how much the liquor was flowing, but now his beard shows a few days of white bristly growth, his hands too tremorous to shave.

He looks back at the house for a minute, then out-ward over the yard, from neighbor to neighbor, and down to the street. She's hidden in the leaves above his sightline.

His face is perplexed and far away, but then that's quickly replaced by a look of purpose. He angles his body over his club, adjusts his stance, looks toward the Millers' hedge, and swings, swooshing over the damp grass, watching the phantom ball rise high into the air.

"You're pulling your swing at the end," Grace says.

He freezes.

"Dad."

He looks around, spooked.

"Callie?" he asks quietly.

"It's Grace," she says, impatiently rolling her eyes. "Up here. In the tree."

"What the hell?" he says. "What're you doing?"

"I couldn't sleep," she offers as explanation.

He glances quickly to where his ball might have landed, then back to his daughter.

"It's in the spinach," she says.

He chuckles, leaning on his club, winded.

"Are you coming down?"

She doesn't answer.

"Hmm?"

"I can't."

He laughs a little and starts to cough, wagging his head. With an awkward gait, he makes it to the base of the maple and mumbles something unintelligible.

"What?"

"The grass," he says. "Needs to be cut."

"Looks okay from up here," she says.

He smiles a little with one side of his mouth. She tries to warm her toes in her hands, her back wedged against a branch.

"Wait there," he says, and then laughs again.

"Ha ha," she says.

He heads slowly back to the garage, his bed-tousled hair going every which way.

He emerges a few minutes later dragging a ladder behind him, plodding across the grass. There is a sheen on his brow and his breath rattles. He puts his hand on the trunk and hangs his head in exhaustion.

"Dad, why don't you go rest. Mom can help me down."

He extends the ladder on the ground, and then hoists it up against the trunk.

He wheezes.

"Dad."

"I have it," he growls, securing the feet of the ladder.

Somehow she turns herself around, grazing her cheek against the bark, and finds a rung with her foot. Her legs are stiff and her arms shake as she inches her way down. He steps away as she approaches. Her shirt is torn and her face bleeds.

"What a mess," he says.

She combs the detritus from her hair with her fingers.

"Go on home," he says between exhales.

Home meaning inside, meaning New York, meaning away from him? She doesn't ask. She takes the ladder and collapses it, but when she tries to carry it, he pulls it gruffly from her hands.

# # #

"It made it easier for me when Caroline was born," Charles says. "She's four years younger than me. I could tell my parents were relieved. My mom used to dress her up in little outfits. But I was always glad to have her. I miss her a lot."

Grace sits in her dad's den, coiled up in his armchair.

"I once had a sister, too," she says. "Callie. She died when she was eight. I was ten."

"Oh, that's too bad," he says, his voice slow and distant.

"But I think it was the same for my parents. She was a second chance or something. She made it all better."

"What was she like?"

"Outgoing. Cute. Spunky."

"Sounds like Caroline. It's like she and I weren't related. Sarah was like them," he says.

Grace waits, but he doesn't go any further.

"I was thinking about Ohio," he says. "I wish I could have appreciated it more. The good parts about it."

"That's always the way it is though, isn't it?"

"For a place I couldn't wait to leave, I would give a lot to be there now," he says.

His longing settles heavily between them. She hears a guard yell.

"I should've asked for help," he says.

She sits up.

"What do you mean? When?"

"When I knew something was going wrong. But it was gradual and I was used to it. I didn't think anyone else could understand. I thought it would get easier at college. I thought I could start over and no one would be able to tell. But I guess that didn't turn out so well."

Their call is interrupted by the loud tones of numbers being dialed.

"Mom, I'm on the phone," Grace yells. The phone goes quiet.

"Charles, what happened at Emeryville?" she asks.

"I can't talk about that."

"Okay. Maybe you can tell me something about when you were a kid."

"It wasn't all bad," he says. "We went to Sea World once."

Grace smiles. The four of them went there once, too. She and Callie had played on the pirate ship jungle gym, climbing rope ladders and sliding down the masts, as her mom watched and her dad slipped off to the beer garden. At the killer whale show, she got jealous when Callie was chosen to touch Shamu's nose.

"It was really hot and sunny," Charles says. "We drank lemonade and ate fried shrimp from little cardboard boats. Caroline got a stuffed penguin and I got a bottle with a ship in it. At the diving tank, my dad bought my mom an oyster with a pearl inside. Nothing that exciting, I guess. But I remember being happy. I was bummed when I heard they'd closed it down."

"It's probably better that way," she says. "If you went back to see it now I'm sure it would seem a little grim."

"Seeing how things are going, I probably wouldn't have been able to see it again anyway," he says.

⚡ ⚡ ⚡

"Grace," her mother says, finding her sprawled on the couch with her hand over her eyes. "Are you okay?"

"Yeah."

"Are you depressed?"

"No," Grace says. "It's just my winning personality."

"You forget who you're talking to. You weren't always this dour. You were an effervescent child."

Her mother sits on the edge of the couch and shines her glasses on the tail of her shirt.

"You're thinking of the wrong daughter," Grace says, squinting against the sunlight.

"I'm serious, Grace."

"Come on, Mom." Her head hurts.

"There's wine gone, your father said."

Grace sits up to a terrible head rush.

"Are you trying to ask me something, or are you just making idle commentary?"

"It's certainly not me drinking it," her mother says.

Grace laughs.

"Thanks for clearing that up."

"Grace."

"*Mother*. Like father, like daughter, I guess."

Her mother sets her jaw.

"I'm so sorry to have depleted the stash," Grace says. "You know, just because he isn't on skid row drinking Thunderbird from a bag doesn't mean it isn't a problem."

"Don't be patronizing and don't change the subject. It's your well-being that concerns me," her mother says in measured tones.

Grace shakes her head but keeps quiet.

"You don't know everything, you know," her mother says.

Neither do you, Grace thinks.

She looks at her mother's birdlike hands, her wedding ring loose on her finger.

"I have to go," Grace says.

"I could use some olive oil," her mother says. "If you don't mind stopping while you're out."

Grace drives over to Hunter, again to the Raggatts', and parks the car a little before their driveway. There seems to be no one home, but then a Jeep rushes by and pulls in, blaring music and spewing the little pebbles of the driveway onto the lawn. A fit blond girl in track pants and a sweaty sports bra, her hair pulled messily back in a ponytail, jumps down from the passenger side. She is un-selfconscious, with a shadow of coltish clumsiness.

"Hey, is it both pages in precalc?" Caroline yells above the thumping bass. "The homework?"

The driver, a girl with wild, curly brown hair, turns down the music and says something Grace can't make out. There is a peace symbol hanging from her rearview mirror.

"No way. He's way too hot for her. Call me, okay? Later," Caroline says, and waves.

The driver flashes a V with her fingers.

As Caroline swings her bag over her shoulder, she angles just enough to slightly register Grace's presence in the car, the swiftest dark glimmer.

Grace wonders if here in Hunter everyone knows—Charles Sr.'s colleagues, Caroline's classmates, Kathy's book club members—or if they have managed to keep the news quiet. Maybe the Raggatts receive hushed *we know it's not true* support from their friends, palatable alliances until the Raggatts become marked as a murderer's family, courting stares, accusations, double takes.

After Callie died, they became a family with a story, the recipients of forced solemnity and nervous apologies. *There's the family that lost a child.* Grace thinks about Sarah Shafer's family and wonders if they will ever not be viewed with sympathy and horror.

The Jeep, its driver resting her foot up on the open window, barrels by again and Caroline lopes toward the house.

"Excuse me," Grace yells.

Caroline stops and turns back.

Grace scrambles out of the car and up the driveway, without a plan. Caroline's face is young and without lines or blemishes. Her cheeks glow ruddy.

"Hi," Grace says.

"Can I help you?"

Now that Grace is here she wants to stall, at a loss for what to ask.

"Um, yes, I think so."

The girl smiles and leans her head in encouragement.

"I'm sorry to spring on you like this," Grace says. "But

I wanted to talk to you. I want to talk about Charles."

"What?" Caroline says. Her face goes pale.

"I'm not a reporter."

"You have to go," she says, her lip trembling.

"I know that he isn't capable of what they say. I'm sure you don't believe it either."

"He didn't know what he was doing," Caroline says. "He's sick." It is what she has been told, what she has to believe. "I can't talk to you."

"I'm on your side," Grace says. "I'm on his side. I just want to talk. He needs you."

"How dare you?" Caroline's voice is high and thin. "Who are you, even? What do you know about my brother?"

"I just—"

"Get out of here, or I'll call the police."

Caroline hardens her face and walks backwards. She runs into the house and slams the door.

The Raggatts' house is a manicured and still fortress, the windows reflecting the last of the sun.

## CHAPTER 16

It's piercing, a buzzing whine, almost electronic, incessant. The cicadas are back this summer. You can't see them but you hear them everywhere. They're almost loud enough to drown out the laughter of the neighborhood kids playing a game of water-gun tag at the Harrisons' down the street. You covet those sounds, ache for them, haunted by what it must feel like to be a part of them. You are nine years old. You laze on the sprinkler-wet grass under the hot sun. Despite the heat, you are in sweatpants because you don't want to be reminded that you are chubby, that your thighs rub together. The air is heavy and damp. You are the only one home.

You stare hard at the branches of the buckeye tree in the backyard. They are up there, the cicadas. Bulging red eyes. Short stubby antennae. But the wings are delicate and see-

through, like lace or a dried-out leaf when all that's left is the veins. You narrow your focus to one section, one twig, but the cicadas are too well camouflaged. You move to an oak but the branches are too high up to see anything.

You imagine what it's like for them, all the same, calling out together, looking down on the neighborhood. You spin around until you're dizzy and fall to your knees. When everything straightens out, you find a stick and poke around the yard, looking for one that might have strayed and gotten lost.

You don't find a live one, but you do find an abandoned brown cicada skin clinging to the bark of a tree. You pluck it off and cradle the scratchy husk in your palm. Inside the house, the air conditioning gives you goose bumps—your dad likes it freezing—so you take a seat in the kitchen, in the sun, with a bag of Oreos.

You hear a car on the gravel driveway, the engine turn off, two car doors slam, your sister's little feet slapping along the pathway to the house. You didn't want to go to the pool—the kids, the games, your large pale body, the chlorine that stings your eyes.

Your mom likes to go to the pool and wear a bathing suit because she looks better than the other moms. She does aerobics all spring to get ready. If she goes in, she doesn't get her hair wet. She says the chlorine's bad for it but you know that's not the reason. You remember when she used to take you in with your water wings, her hands firm under your arms, face to face, before you got too big and she didn't like that you still wanted her to pull you around.

Your mom comes into the kitchen wearing a bright lime green sundress over her bathing suit, her large sunglasses that make her look like a fly are perched on top of her head. She's drinking a Diet Coke. She finds you chewing with your chin resting on the table.

"Sit up, Charles," she says, taking the cookies away. "How about some carrots." But then she sees you're looking eye to eye with your insect find. She screws up her face. "What is that? A locust? Ick. What are you doing with that? Take it outside."

Caroline shrieks and runs upstairs in her pink bathing suit. She just turned five last week. She is a soft caramel-corn color from a summer at the pool.

"It's not a locust," you say. "It's a cicada."

"I don't care," your mother says, her eyebrows raised. "It's disgusting and it doesn't belong in the house."

You take your cicada shell up to your room and set it on the carpet next to you as you open up the C Encyclopedia. You learn that there's fossil evidence of cicadas from 65 million years ago and the ancient Greeks kept them as pets. Maybe you'll catch one and keep it, you think. But the noise would probably keep you awake at night. A cicada can chirp so loud you can hear it from half a mile away.

"Charles," Caroline says in the doorway, "I swam halfway across underwater without stopping."

You take the insect body and thrust it at her with a monster growl. She screams and laughs and runs away, slamming her bedroom door down the hall.

You learn that male cicadas create their song by vibrating drum-like membranes on their abdomen. They're calling for a mate. But once they mate, they die. You wonder why they look for a mate at all if it's going to kill them. You'd think they would have figured it out by now. Or maybe they hope this time will be different.

You hear your father's car in the driveway. He opens the front door and you listen for where he is in the house, first in the kitchen talking to your mom, and then walking up the stairs. He passes by your room, but comes back. You know he's making himself do it, but at least he has come back and you are glad.

"What're you reading about, champ?"

You warm to the old nickname he never uses anymore since you suck at sports and don't care about bats or balls. You wonder if this will be the last time he calls you this.

"Cicadas," you say. "Did you know that some people eat them?"

"Oh," he says. "No, I didn't. That's something."

Your father is looking out the window when he says this. He doesn't like to look at you. His face is sunburned. He was out sailing on Lake Erie today but he didn't invite you along. He squats down next to you but doesn't sit.

"Did you ever hear the story about the cicada?" he asks.

You shake your head, thrilled to have him to yourself, soaking up his presence in your room even though you know he is biding his time before he can go.

"During the summer, the ant worked hard to gather food for the coming winter. But the cicada sang and made fun of the ant for working so hard. When the winter came, the cicada had nothing to eat and had to beg the ant for food," he says.

"But ants don't eat the same things as cicadas," you say, confused by the story.

"No, it's a fable. It's not supposed to be real."

"Oh," you say. "Okay."

You smile too widely and laugh, trying to make him happy.

"Do you understand? It's a story with a moral. Don't put off until tomorrow what you should do today."

"Yeah. It's good to do stuff right away," you say.

Your dad smiles without smiling.

"Yeah," he says. "Kind of."

"Dad!" Caroline calls from down the hall. "Daddy!"

"Coming, pumpkin," he says.

You turn back to your book as your dad leaves. After mating, the female cicada cuts slits into the bark of a branch and deposits her eggs. When the eggs hatch, the newborn nymphs drop to the ground, where they burrow in the dirt to begin another cycle. When they've matured, they build an exit tunnel to the surface and emerge into the world. They shed their skins, and they are adults.

You forgot all about your specimen and now you see that your dad has accidentally crushed the dried body with his shoe. Three legs are buried in the carpet. The torso is split in half. You gather up the remains and place them on your dresser like it's an operating table. But the Elmer's comes out too fast, drowning the leg you are trying to glue back on. You try to wipe it off on your sweatpants but then your fingers stick together and the cicada leg breaks in half. Glue oozes out from the overturned bottle and globs onto the carpeting. You will yourself not to cry. Don't be a baby, you think. You pound your fist against your leg. You stupid baby.

You scoop up the hull fragments in your hand, take them into your bathroom, and flush them down the toilet. One brown, spiny leg floats in the bowl.

Outside, the chorus whines. You run as fast as you can across the big lawn, arms out, face up toward the sun, pumping your stocky legs, trying to get away from yourself.

But then you run out of breath and have to stop. You don't feel any lighter. You feel the same.

After the stabbing had taken place, police believe Raggatt wrapped Shafer's body in plastic bags and placed it in his Land Rover, where the body remained for seven days. He then moved the body and buried it in the backyard of a property at Long Beach, a place he was renting.

"I don't think there is any rational interpretation," Mr. Dubno said. "But that is not the issue. The issue is, is he responsible for what he did? Is he legally responsible? And I think that is going to be answered in the negative."

## CHAPTER 17

It is a brilliant day, the warmest yet. The sky is corn-flower blue, the air velvety from pollen and evaporating dew. Despite her botched run-in with Caroline, Grace wakes up feeling energized by purpose, newly committed. Her notebook pages bulge with scrawled notes, and she feels buoyed by the possibility of discovery, the rightness of her search.

She finds her mother in back of the house, kneeling between rows of tomato plants.

"Do you need any help?" Grace asks.

"Oh hi, Grace," her mother says, sitting up on her heels. She brushes the hair off her face and unknowingly smears dirt across her forehead. "No. I'm okay."

"What's Dad up to?"

"He's at the slides again. He got out the tray from our

famous canoe trip."

"The photos make it *look* like we had fun," Grace says and laughs.

"Oh come on, we had fun," her mother says, her eyes hopeful as she stands and stretches her back.

"Yeah, I guess," Grace says, wondering what her mother has chosen to remember.

Her father had been in a sour mood the morning they set out in the car for a river in southern Ohio, hungover and distant behind his aviator sunglasses, his hair lightened from the summer sun. Her mother, in a white shirt and khaki Bermudas, held a large picnic basket on her lap like she was holding a child, smiling back at Grace and Callie, her dark hair kerchiefed from her tanned face. They had all been looking forward to this trip for weeks.

Despite the early hour, her dad drank four beers from his chilled six-pack on the drive down. Grace and Callie, already in their bathing suits, their thighs sticking to the vinyl of the backseat, baited each other across an imaginary dividing line. Callie tattled on Grace for touching her and their dad yelled at Grace to behave. In the front, their parents snipped at each other.

But by the time they got into the canoe, strapped into their bulging orange life vests, their dad's spirits had brightened and he was the playful man his daughters adored. To their delight, he splashed them as he oared, and for a gilded moment, they floated on calm, dappled water. He looked over his shoulder and smiled at his wife, roping her in, and she smiled back. Everything, it seemed, was right.

They stopped at a little island, where they skipped rocks after a lunch of crustless peanut butter sandwiches, chocolate chip cookies, and apple juice from a thermos, but Grace and Callie soon grew groggy and restless. Back in the canoe with so many miles to go, their parents started rowing faster, complaining about sore arms and the other's crooked paddling. The beer ran out too soon. Callie threw a tantrum over not getting a chance to row. Their father gave in to her, as he always did, and as he stood to switch places, he lost his balance and the boat capsized, dumping them all into the water.

"Jesus Christ!" he screamed.

"Jack!" their mother hissed back at him, miraculously holding the camera above the water.

Her bra showed through her wet shirt and mascara ran down her cheek.

Callie started crying, which turned into red-faced sobbing. Grace told her to shut up and was quickly scolded by her mother. The picnic basket floated away in the current until it got stuck on some tree roots down-river. Her father's wallet was a soaked brown square.

"Where are my goddamn keys? Goddamnit. The car keys."

"Jack, please," her mother said, quietly furious.

"Susan, I don't want to hear it from you. This trip was your idea."

They all peered into the water. Grace wanted to be the one to find the keys, to salvage something from the day, to win back her father. The canoe filled with water and sank. Her mother waded off to rescue the picnic basket.

"I found them!"

Callie jumped up and down in the water, jingling the keys above her head, her cheeks still glistening from tears.

"That's my girl," their dad said, patting her sun-warmed head.

With the help of passing teenagers, the canoe was emptied and righted, and they were back on their soggy way.

Memory is a finicky chronicler. Grace's mother seems only to remember a snapshot of the four of them together in the boat, before they capsized, before Callie died.

Grace pulls apart the yellow tuft of a dandelion. Her mother resumes her weeding, unearthing a good-sized stone from the dirt.

"What are you going to do today, Grace?"

"More research. I have to make use of my time here."

Her mother glances at her.

"You think that boy didn't do it? Is that it?"

"I think he was bullied into a confession. He wanted to please people. I think he just gave up."

"I only know what you've told me about it, but what about the police?" her mother asks.

Grace shakes her head dismissively.

"I mean, he knew the girl. He liked her. I think he felt guilty for something. But I don't think he did what they accuse him of. He's a good kid, Mom. Damaged. But not evil."

Grace picks a lavender flower from the myrtle ground-cover, sucking on it for any trace of honey. There is a faint sweetness.

"Isn't that his lawyer's job?" her mother asks, shading her eyes with her gloved hand. "To explain what happened?"

"It should be. But people believe what they want to believe. They're going with an insanity plea."

"So you think he *might* have killed the girl?"

Grace rubs her hands over her face.

"I don't know," she says finally. "Maybe he was a witness. Or it was an accident. But whatever happened, he's not willing to fight for himself."

She picks another flower and a bumblebee the size of a kumquat flies at her, buzzing around her head as she zigzags away.

"Just stand still and it'll go away," her mother says.

"Easy for you to say."

Grace runs a circle around the garden.

"I'm just trying to understand, Grace. About what

you're doing."

When Grace stops running, the bee flies away.

"You're the one who used to say, 'Love the sinner not the sin.' He needs my help," Grace says. "And there isn't anyone else."

Her mother sets her trowel down and wipes a lock of hair from her forehead with her wrist. Her mouth opens to speak but nothing comes out.

"I'm going to get the mail," Grace says. "Do you have anything to go out?"

"No, but your father might. You should go ask him."

Grace purses her lips at the thought.

"Oh, Grace?"

"Yeah?"

"I almost forgot, a nice boy called this morning for you."

"What?" Her mind trips over itself.

"Brian something in New York. His number's on the fridge."

"Brian." She exhales with puffed-out cheeks.

Her mom wants to ask, as another mother might, if he is a suitor or has that potential. But she's not one to initiate conspiratorial conversation. She has always been rather Protestant in her reticence to pry into Grace's business.

"He's just my boss," Grace tosses out as she walks toward the house.

She pours herself a glass of her dad's tomato juice,

forgoing the splash of vodka that she wants, and takes the phone into the family room, falling into the unyielding leather couch with a squeak. She dials.

"Brian. Hi, it's Grace."

She feels tentative and shy. She sips her juice and hopes he has moved past the kiss.

"Grace, hi!" he beams. "Thanks for calling me back."

She's a little touched; it's not like she's been gone very long.

"Of course," she says. "How are you?"

"I'm good. How are *you*? I mean, your dad? Is he okay?"

"He's okay. Getting better," she says.

"That's great. I'm really glad to hear it."

"So what's up?"

From the back window Grace can see into the woods, abloom with leaves and buds. She used to think they went on forever, that within them were mysteries to discover, secret spots that no one else had found. The first time she made it through to the other side and came out in a back-yard on Donner Street, she was heartsick. There was an end to everything.

"I just wanted to see how you were doing," he says.

"Really?"

Brian laughs. "Yeah, is that so weird?"

"No, no. That's nice," she says. "How is it there?"

"Busy. I'm eagerly awaiting your return. I took for

granted how quick you are at plowing through stuff. We're lagging without you."

"I'll be back soon," she says, taking a big swallow of her breakfast.

She spins her watch around to see the time, but she has forgotten to wind it again.

"Good. Okay," he says. "I'm off to a meeting. If you need anything, let me know."

"Okay," she smiles.

She wanders through the quiet house, its windows cracked to the spring air and sounds of twittering sparrows. As she nears her father's den, she hears him muttering to himself and stops outside the door.

"Damnit to hell," he grumbles.

He is sitting on the floor, still in his pajamas, surrounded by a mess of slides and round plastic trays.

"Shit," he says.

He holds a slide up to the light of the window and with fumbling fingers, tries to fit it into a slot of the tray, only to lose hold of it. Again and again he tries, cursing his clumsiness. And then he pulls a bottle of whiskey from his desk drawer, and, gripping it by its neck, drinks straight from the bottle. One, two, three seconds, down his gullet as if it's water and he's just in from the desert.

The image stings. It's not the baseness of the gesture, but its urgency. She saw it once before when she was a teenager. He had topped off his drink at the bar and there were a couple inches left in the bottle. Thinking he was alone, he brought it to his mouth and emptied it back, wiping his mouth with his arm like she had seen done in an old western. Now he is white-haired and angry, unable to make his fingers work. He screws the cap back on with effort, before shutting the bottle back in the drawer.

"Hi, Dad," she says.

It takes him a moment to place her, to return from wherever he has been.

"Hi," he says, looking back to the disarray in front of him.

"What are you working on?"

"Organizing," he says. "Been meaning to do it for a long time."

"Do you need help?" she asks, not wanting to but wanting him to say yes.

"No," he says, shaking his head. "No."

"I'm going out to the mailbox if you need anything mailed."

"I'm making a Callie tray," he says. "The highlights. Zero to eight."

"Oh," she nods.

The light from the window makes a square on his chest.

"Maybe my highlight tray will be your summer project," she says.

He looks up at her.

"Or maybe it'll be more than one tray, since I have so many more years," she chirps. "A highlight tray set."

Her father opens and closes his mouth like a fish.

"Maybe you'll include a picture of me when I was thirteen with Hank Morgenstern. He'll be smiling in it. And his hand will be on my thigh."

Her dad grunts and looks past her to the doorway for some kind of escape. She wants a reaction, an admission, a defense, anything. But his face is an illegible map of anxiety, pain, and confusion. He will not let her in.

"Okay," she says, defeated.

He looks down at the slides, a sea of jigsaw puzzle pieces around him.

"So nothing for the mail then?"

He doesn't answer.

She leaves him to his mining of the past.

CHAPTER 18

Grace cleans out her mother's spice rack, tossing doubles (cloves, allspice, thyme) and crusty ten-year-old containers (poultry seasoning, tarragon, marjoram). She walks out to the mailbox, ready to run back if the phone rings. She examines her face in the bathroom mirror and over-plucks her eyebrows. She fears that he will never call again.

# # #

"I got a letter today from an anonymous person in New Jersey. I'll read you what it says. 'Charles Raggatt, you are inhuman and every day I pray that you will receive the death penalty, your just reward.'"

"Why doesn't your lawyer counteract the stories that get put out? I don't get it," Grace says.

"He's doing what he thinks is best. What my parents

think is best for me."

"I don't think the D.A. will seek the death penalty."

"I'm told it's a real possibility," Charles says.

"That won't happen," she says. "If people under-stand."

"Have you ever had the feeling that you were suffo-cating?" he asks.

"Sometimes I feel like I'm drowning, like I'm being sucked under. I'm caught between wanting to get above it and the urge to just give in."

"What do you do," he asks, "when you feel that way?"

"Usually I take the easy way out and drink myself into oblivion. So I don't have to choose."

"I used to knock my head into a wall. Or burn myself with matches. I crashed my car once."

"Your parents never noticed that you did these things?"

"No one's ever looking that hard," he says. There's a loud buzzer in the background and a man yells. "Sorry for the noise. It's never quiet here. I wish for real quiet. I wish for a lot of things."

"Like what?"

He doesn't answer.

"Charles?"

"I wish we could each have one do-over. To use when-ever we wanted."

"You're not alone," she says.

"Grace?"

"Yeah?"

"The fact that they are calling this a premeditated murder…it's just not true."

"I believe you," she says. He doesn't respond. "I believe you. Let me help you."

"I was thinking last night," he says, "when I couldn't sleep, about a book I read first semester for English. Have you heard of *The Myth of Sisyphus*?"

"I read it in college but that was fifteen years ago."

"I can't say I really understood it that well, but there was something that stuck with me and it's become more important to me here in jail, because every day looks the same. He says in the book that we should imagine Sisyphus happy, that in the absence of hope, we have to struggle to survive."

"Charles, tell me what happened."

"Were you ever jealous of your sister?" he asks.

"All the time. We didn't get along that well. I didn't like her very much. Sometimes we had fun together but usually we fought. She liked to get me into trouble."

"Parents like to pretend they don't play favorites but they do," he says. "They don't even hide it that well."

"I think it's one of the reasons Callie didn't think anything bad could happen. She didn't worry because she knew everyone was looking out for her."

Charles sighs. His words are muffled.

"What?"

"I never felt like anyone was looking out for me," he says.

"This is awful to say, but when my sister died, part of me thought: so there."

"Grace?"

"Yeah?"

"Sometimes you remind me of me. Not that I'd wish that on anybody."

*# *# *#

Hunter High School is a large, turn-of-the-century brick building with a vaguely gothic façade. Grace parks in the visitors' lot in the shade of a beech tree and watches the students spill out of Charles's old school, laughing groups of shiny kids, boys in varsity jackets, girls in expensive jeans. She tries to imagine him, one step behind, looking for the signs of how to act written in a language he couldn't learn. Always askew.

Charles's sister emerges from a side door in a three-some of girls, her head back in unbridled laughter as she ambles across the lawn. She has a glow about her, a true-ness. Grace wonders if Caroline wants to talk to Charles or if she has given up on him. Maybe she doesn't want to know. Grace scrunches down in the seat, out of view.

And then as she is leaned over, staring at the glove compartment, she understands what should have been so obvious. If it were her, and she had checked into a run-down motel by herself, it would have meant she felt bad and wanted to feel worse. It would have meant she had had enough. Charles went to the Econo Lodge in Hickton to kill himself. He checked in with a knife to put an end to the spiraling disaster of his year at Emeryville, in the anonymous decay of that room.

When she sits up, Caroline and her friends are gone and only a sprinkle of students idles in front of the building. Grace rolls down the window to the faint rhythmic chanting of cheerleading practice.

She bites her nails. Her head throbs. She's not moving fast enough. She's wasting time here in Ohio.

She drives into town, past the old-fashioned Rexall drug store and the freshly painted white gazebo in the middle of the square where Dixie bands play in the summer and craft shows encamp in fall. A couple of kids toss a Frisbee across the grass. She is definitely in the wrong place.

She heads west, out of the nicer part of town, to an area of strip malls and fast-food restaurants and flimsy apartment complexes offering week-to-week leases. Circles, a bar at the Ramada, isn't open yet. Further out there's a Hooters. She doubles back and pulls into Happy House Lounge and Chinese Restaurant, a stand-alone place that looks like it used to be a Howard Johnson. On the sign there is a smiling face with slashes for eyes. She parks.

When she was sixteen, Grace lost her virginity with a boy from the club in a janitor's closet, after a mixed doubles tennis tournament. It hurt, but she didn't dwell on it. Sex seemed like not that big a deal. It wasn't until college that this changed, that she felt the pull of male attention, the narcotic power of the physical, the lure of a new body. Sex was the space for escape and nullification that she'd been looking for all along.

In the restaurant entryway, striped and colored fishes swim lethargically in the cloudy water of a giant aquarium. Late-afternoon light streams through the front window in a dusty swath across the bar. At one end, an older woman in a purple polyester suit drinks a beer and nibbles fried chow mein noodles, shielding the side of her face from the sun. At the other, in the shadow, is a man in a short-sleeved button-down shirt with closely cropped hair and smooth, muscled arms. Grace can't see his face. She sits one stool away from him and orders a vodka tonic.

Upon closer inspection, when her eyes adjust, the man is quite attractive, with long-lashed hazel eyes, full lips, and amaretto skin. He is drinking a cognac and reading the baseball scores from a folded-over *Plain Dealer*.

"Hello," he says.

"Hi," she says.

"What happened to you?"

Her incident with the tree has left a scab on her cheek, still tender pink around the edges.

"You should see the other guy," she says.

He reaches toward her face and she rears back a little.

"An eyelash," he says.

"Sorry," she says, leaning to let him get it.

"Didn't mean to freak you out," he says.

"You didn't. Cheers."

She holds up her drink.

"Yeah," he says, and laughs a little, clinking her glass. "Bottoms up."

They drink.

"Tom," he says holding out his hand.

"Grace."

He takes her hand and gently squeezes.

"So what do you do?" she asks.

"Retired. From the military. I do a little of this, a little of that. You?" He leers a bit when he says this, as if he knows she is about to lie.

"Race car driver," she says.

"Hah," he laughs, swirling his drink.

Tom buys a bottle of Hennessey from the bartender and they take off into the evening. Even out here, amidst the swooshing of cars, the call of crickets accompanies the darkness. Grace is unusually woozy. The headlights and taillights of passing cars run together in blurry streams.

Tom has offered to get them a room at the Ramada down the street using his military discount, because he claims to live in Lorraine—too far away for them to go back to his place. She doesn't get into particulars because they don't much matter to her. Tom has nice hands, strong and long-fingered. As he pulls his giant Oldsmobile out of the parking lot, bouncing slowly off the curb, she thinks she might be sick.

"I was in Vietnam," he says. "In 1972."

"Oh," she says.

This makes him much older than she'd guessed. She wishes they we were already in bed, in the dark.

"Relationships are hard for me," he says.

Oh God, she thinks, *please be quiet*. She has the spins when she closes her eyes and she's starting to lose her nerve.

The room is salmon-colored and smells of sprayed air freshener. The cheap nylon bedspread is worn in spots and one of the curtains has come off its metal rail. Tom sits on the bed in his clothes and hands her the bottle of cognac, which she drinks out of habit, not even wanting it, the last swallow coming back up.

"I don't feel well," she says, boozily tripping on the end of the bed.

"Why don't you come here," Tom says, holding out his ropey arm toward her.

She goes to him and he pulls her onto the bed. He

grabs her hair and kisses her hard on the mouth.

# # #

The phone rings and rings until finally it stops. Grace rolls over slowly—her brain feels like it is floating loosely in her head. She is naked, except for her socks and her watch, and she is alone. It is three a.m. The bedside light exposes an empty bottle of Hennessey on the floor near her bra and inside-out jeans. Panic gives way to regret, and then to shame. She throws up, first right in the bed, and then again in the bathroom sink. There's a condom floating in the toilet. The mirror shows someone haggard and green, worn out. She can't remember much after arriving in the room.

She sits on the edge of the bed and gingerly dresses, moving slowly, her hands unsteady. She stands but then sits back down and drops her head between her knees. It's too much.

She's still muddled as she trips along the deserted thoroughfare back to the Happy House, stopping once to dry-heave into the weeds. Her mother's car waits alone in the parking lot. She collapses behind the wheel.

When Grace finally turns into Woodland Road, relieved by its stillness, she rolls down the window and takes a deep breath. But then there is a bump under the tire and she lurches the car to a stop. She spills out in the middle of the dark street and the interior light shines on a little mound of fur and blood, claws and teeth. A squirrel. One of its legs jerks, and a dead eye holds her with an accusatory stare.

## CHAPTER 19

"Charles," your mom says. "Come now. I know you can do it. Say ball. Ball."

She rolls the soccer ball to you and it bounces off your shins before you can grasp it. You're too focused on the black hexagons blurring together. You are not coordinated.

"Think how proud Daddy will be," she says, holding the ball up. "Ball."

But you are marveling at the big coils of sod the men are unloading to cover up the dirt in the backyard. Grass comes in rolls! You giggle. Who cares about a black-and-white ball when there are huge spools of grass that men deliver. What they've been telling you is wrong. Grass doesn't grow from seeds after all. It arrives on a truck. Maybe more things they say aren't true either.

"Charles? Sweetie. Say it for Mommy."

Your mom is young and pretty in her pink gingham dress, but she is anxious and weary and you can feel it in the space between you two. You point at the grass carpeting, hoping to distract her from her singular pursuit because you are getting tired and you want to be alone.

"Please don't do this," she says, lacing and unlacing her fingers. "I know you're not dumb."

Your dad thinks you're dumb. He wants to trade you in for another son.

A blue jay lands on the bird feeder and you run on pudgy legs toward it, wanting to hold it in your fat little hands.

"Yes. Bird," she says. "Charles, look at me. Bird."

You look at her but you won't say anything. You smile, wanting to see your mom look happy, wanting her to not push you anymore, to let you be as you are.

"Don't get too close. Jays are mean birds," she says.

The men with the sod have unrolled the last of the grass, covering the mud with soft green. Your mother dreams of the day when the Raggatts will be rich and you will be able to move out of this split-level house. For now she will make the best home for her family, petunias and zinnias along the walkway, meatloaf and green bean casserole in the oven.

She sighs and quickly covers a scowl with a wide-eyed smile when she sees you watching her. The blue jay has flown away. You lie on the grass and look up at the branches of the new willow tree that was delivered and set into the ground by the men. You could stay here for hours.

"Okay then," your mother says. "If that's the way you're going to be. Let's go."

She touches her stomach, a growing hard mound, as she gets up from the grass. She tells you that you are going to have a little sister and you will have to teach her things. You can't wait because then it won't be only up to you anymore. Later you will wonder what would have happened if Caroline had not come along and they had had to deal with only you, but it might not have made any difference anyway.

"Charles, let's go. Get up."

But you don't want to. The clouds keep coming and you don't want to miss one. Moving, splitting, reconnecting. The thin little branches of the new tree are so fragile and they need you here to make sure they withstand the wind. You shake your head "no" against the ground.

"Now," she says, frustrated, through clenched teeth, careful not to alert the yard workers. "Get up this minute." Her eyes are shiny pools. She grabs your arm and pulls but you go limp, refusing. "Do not do this to me."

Her nails dig into your soft arm and a curl of her hair falls loose across her forehead. She is crying now, stifling the sound with a red scrunched face, and although you know you could make it better, you are filling with your own fury, a knot of anger, and you pretend you are a rock and no one can get to you.

She drags you now, despite the glances she gets from the

men loading the shovels onto the truck. Your arm hurts and your head bumps along but you are silent. If you talk, you know you won't ever be able to go back to how it is inside yourself. When she gets you in the house and slams the sliding glass door, she leaves you lying on the floor, watching the ceiling. You fall asleep right there, lulled by the sound of her angry vacuum crisscrossing the living room.

Charles Raggatt pleaded not guilty by reason of mental disease or defect at his arraignment on first-degree murder charges in a Nassau County courtroom this morning. Raggatt is charged with drugging, kidnapping, and stabbing to death fellow student Sarah Shafer last April. Police say he was upset because Shafer rejected his sexual advances.

## CHAPTER 20

Grace has agreed to have dinner with her parents down the street at the Chenowiths'. She would like to behave tonight, to get through it, to leave on an unfraught note and put this visit behind her. She has had enough of Ohio.

Her father wears seersucker pants and a white shirt, and her mother is in a kelly green sweater set. Take away a few wrinkles and add hair color, and it could be twenty-five years ago, the annual kickoff cookout at the club, gin and tonics all around. They walk slowly and carefully, she and her mother flanking her dad like police escorts, down the little incline of Woodland Road to the Chenowiths' gated driveway.

Marjorie answers the door in a linen ensemble with chunky wooden bracelets. She has not aged as well as

Grace's mother, her middle large and her face heavily creased. Grace remembers when Marjorie used to sunbathe in her backyard, slathered in baby oil, her bathing suit straps tucked under her armpits, *Scruples* splayed on her stomach.

"Hi!" she says, kissing Grace's dad and then her mom on the cheek. "Look at you," she says, enveloping Grace in a hug. "Come on in, folks."

The house, as her mother has told her, was redone a few years ago. Grace feels like she has stepped into a design showcase for country chic, complete with pine floors, distressed cabinets, and an enormous stone fireplace. Black-and-white portraits of their kids—two boys and a girl—are hung all over the house. Grace used to baby-sit them when the sunken living room had rust shag carpeting and a sectional couch that wrapped around half the room.

Their yellow lab, Louise, whom she loved as a girl, is long since dead, but a replacement, a little thinner and paler, greets them with tail-thumping interest. And then Mr. Chenowith, Harvey, appears from the back patio in madras pants and a panama hat, with wide arms and a loud "Look who's here!"

Aside from being her mother's maybe-paramour, he was the neighborhood flirt, always telling the women how beautiful they looked and the girls what heartbreakers they were sure to be, pulling them onto his lap, well past the age of appropriateness.

He picks Grace up in a hug and she's afraid he might start tickling her like he used to. He is an avuncular version of his old pervy self.

"You lucky girl, getting your mother's looks," he says.

"Jackson," he says to her father with mock seriousness. "We need you back out there on the course. Newton is pulling us all down with him."

They pump hands and Harvey slaps him on the shoulder.

"Gorgeous, as usual," he says to her mother, who shakes her head at him but smiles.

Once, when Grace was babysitting here, she found a *Hustler* magazine in their bedside table while snooping around after putting the kids to bed. She was twelve. Hers was not a naked household like some were. She had never seen a penis. She knew the biological basics of sex, mainly from the *Where Do Babies Come From?* film they showed in school, but she was still a kid.

On the cover of the issue was the face of a woman in a box with the title "Giving Head," the meaning of which was entirely lost on Grace. Inside there was the Hustler Honey Centerfold on a chaise lounge, sitting knees up, spread-eagled. "Beaver Hunt" featured readers who sent in "snatchshots" taken by their boyfriends. There were cartoons about child molesters that she didn't understand but made her blush anyway. Photo upon photo of vaginas, penises, insouciant bodies. She was fascinated and repulsed and confused and riveted. Each image in the magazine was etched into her memory. She felt like she had peeked through a window into the secret lives of adults.

When the Chenowiths returned that night, Grace was too ashamed to look them in the eye. She thought that when Mr. Chenowith drove her home, he would say something because he could tell. Although she only saw the magazine that one night—it was gone the next time she looked—she's afraid that no amount of chintz and old farmhouse furniture will make her remember this place any differently.

"Okay, what'll it be?" Harvey bellows, shaking his already empty glass of ice toward them.

He tends to the libations with expert quickness, erring on the strong side. With drinks in hand, they go out back where a plate of steaks rests next to the smoking grill.

The sun has fallen behind the western woods, filtering through the branches and new foliage. The sky above is inky blue. Fireflies begin to wink. Grace excuses herself, refreshes her vodka tonic, and takes a stroll around the expansive yard, shoes in hand, the grass cool and soft. The dog trots along somewhere behind her. The backyard slopes down with a curve—one of her and Callie's favorite sledding places—and they have since put in a pool, not yet uncovered for the season. She hears a child cry and peers through the hedge to next door. There's a large swing set in a state of half-installation where the Meltzers' badminton court used to be, before they filed for bankruptcy and fled to Arizona.

# # #

By the time the strawberries with Devonshire cream come around for dessert, Grace is stuffed and her head swims. Marjorie is talking about her youngest, Scott, who graduated from Princeton and has joined Morgan Stanley as an analyst in Boston but she hopes will settle a little closer to home.

"Oh wouldn't that be great if he moved back to Cleveland?" Grace's mother chimes in.

Grace wonders if her mother ever had a secret life of her own. An affair with Harvey Chenowith, smoking cigarettes, an amorous pen pal, shoplifting candy bars, visiting the hospital nursery, writing sestinas. Something that was hers alone.

Alcohol loosens Grace's father's stubborn speech but he's still not comfortable with his thickened tongue. He stares off into the dark.

Harvey takes it upon himself to liven things up.

"So, Ms. Grace," he says. "Do you have a boyfriend out there in New York City?"

He raises his eyebrows together in quick succession.

Her mom giggles and says, "Good luck getting anything out of her, Harvey."

"No," Grace says, laughing a little.

She feels the breeze on her neck and she shifts in her seat, the iron of the chair now cold.

"No? Come on, give me a little something here," he says, shaking her shoulder. "Tell us about your romantic adventures."

"What, do you want to know about my sex life?" she asks.

"Grace," her mother says, shooting her a stern look.

"Now we're talking," Harvey says, and claps his hands.

"You know the Stevensons," Marjorie says to the table as she scrapes the remains of the desserts into her bowl. "Their son Rob is in New York, I think. He's probably about your age, Grace. A lawyer. Not married."

"She's not interested in normal things," her father slurs.

"What?" Grace asks.

He finishes his latest drink.

"Look what you're missing out on," Harvey says, opening his arms wide with barely veiled irony. "Don't you want to get married, buy a house, have kids?"

"Keep *Hustler* in the bedside table?" Grace asks.

Marjorie drops a fork, sending a splash of strawberry-stained cream across her sandaled foot.

"I was dating someone for a while," Grace adds. "But he was married." Her mother's face goes taught. "Now I just stick to casual sex."

"Jesus, Grace," her mother says, as Harvey laughs.

"That's the spirit," he says.

Her dad looks at her with drunk, bitter eyes.

"What?" she asks, sloshed too.

"Nothing," he says, opening his palms to her. "It's your life."

"How about you, Mr. Chenowith? Any philandering you'd like to catch us up on?"

He laughs but stops.

"Or maybe you want to answer that one, Mom?"

"Okay, then," her mother says standing. "Marjorie, Harvey, thank you."

Her chair scrapes against the brick as she moves to go.

Grace lurches ahead.

"Callie would have been different, right Dad?" she asks him, quietly. "She never would have ruined a perfectly nice evening."

He looks at her, startled. Something passes between them, imperceptible to everyone else.

"The good thing is that we won't remember this tomorrow," Harvey says.

"Speak for yourself, Harvey," Marjorie mutters, getting up.

"I'll see you two at home," Grace's mother says.

"Susan, I'll walk you," Marjorie says, pulling her sweater from the back of the chair.

The women disappear down the dark driveway.

"Shall the rest of us retire inside for a nightcap?" Harvey asks, snuffing out the last remaining lit candle nub. "Maybe Grace can enlighten us on other subjects."

"I'm going for a walk," Grace says, stumbling, as she catches her heel on the chair.

"Better take your training wheels, young lady," Harvey says.

She leaves the men in the glow of the light from the kitchen.

"No one gives a shit about the truth," she says as she nears the end of the driveway, but the night swallows her words and the men have already gone inside.

## CHAPTER 21

Y*ou have said to your mother, "Please don't," but she just smiles and says, "It'll be so much fun," in that hopeful, cheery voice, the same one she uses to turn down the phone solicitors who call during dinner. She has hired a caterer, and oddly, a carnival supply company, as if you are still a child and there is time to fix you, to set you straight, to make you normal. The only people you could rightly invite would be Steve and Kelly, and you could casually mention it to Hadley, but instead your mom has managed to invite your entire class as a graduation celebration. If you think about it too much it becomes a scary montage of garish faces laughing at you. Your dad is not involved with the planning except for shelling out the dough.*

You feel the old eggbeater at work in your head, stirring up the morass of drift, failure, and confusion. And anger. Al-

ways anger.

You want to hide, you want to be gone, you want to disintegrate like those swirling flocks of birds that move as one but then scatter into a million tiny points. You want to shake your mom, that nice lady who gave birth to you and your impossible desires. Mess up her neat hair, destroy her ordered house, kick her until she calls off the party through broken teeth and bloody lips.

You're able to stuff the violence back in a cage. And instead you masturbate to you and Hadley on the hood of your car. But it doesn't work all the way and you get limp and you sneak out to your BMW and fly through the contained suburban streets.

Downtown. Dirty and mean and pulsing with filthy life. You go west to where the dealers and the whores troll, and in your fancy car you circle the decaying blocks and their vile humanity looking for something, anything.

Yeah, you've got forty bucks to get off with her ugly vacant mouth and you feel the tide of heat and anger rise in you once again, her small neck so close to your fat hands choking the steering wheel. You wonder if this makes you no longer a virgin.

Then you drive home and nothing has changed but at least you are exhausted. You fall asleep curled up on the floor beneath your window and focus on how you will reinvent yourself at Emeryville College. You will be thin and handsome and comfortable and smooth. You will fit.

## CHAPTER 22

Grace used to go for months—and one time in her twenties, for years—not thinking of Callie's death. Of the car. The glare. The blood. These days, it's more and more like an infected wound, deepening, itching, burning. Her life careened off-track at the moment of impact. She remembers there was a woodpecker, the tap-tap-tap of its beak against an oak trunk in the background, underneath the call of the cicadas. She remembers that Mr. Jablonski, the old widower who lived in the only small house on the street, had already driven by once that day, probably on the way to one of his church meetings. She had a fiery sunburn on her back from falling asleep under the sprinkler. The night before she had been awakened by the sound of her parents fighting, their words spit and hurled, then her mom crying. She tiptoed to Callie's room but, as usual, her sister just slept right through it. She remembers thinking that if there were a fire, she wouldn't help Callie down the rope ladder that was kept in a trunk in her closet, that Callie would be on her own.

#

"I haven't told my lawyer I talk to you. He wouldn't be too happy if he found out. He doesn't want me to talk to anyone."

Charles sounds low today, like getting the words out requires tremendous effort.

"What about what you want?" Grace asks.

"That hasn't always been the best guide."

"It still matters."

"Do you know what death method they use in New York?"

"You shouldn't think about it."

Lethal injection, she thinks.

"If I'm sentenced to die, I hope I can figure out a way to kill myself before they can," he says.

"Charles, I've had times when I've thought about that kind of thing. Am I high enough if I jumped? Am I going fast enough if I crashed? It's terrible to think like that."

"It's especially hard in the late afternoon, just before the sun starts to set. Even though I'm glad I can see the sky through my tiny window, I'm anxious about the darkness. Dr. Jerry said that the stress of the approaching trial wreaks havoc on a person's emotions. He said he's seen inmates hallucinate."

Charles inhales, and then exhales before continuing.

"You've seen her picture, right?"

Grace starts at this shift to Sarah.

"Yes," she says.

"It probably didn't even do her justice. It wasn't only that she was beautiful, or that I was into her, but she gave off light or something. It's hard to describe."

Silence.

"Charles?"

"It's hard for me to talk about her."

"I know."

"It's not like the papers said. We did know each other. I thought she knew me better that anyone had before. I thought, *finally*," he says.

"Did you two hang out together?"

"At first I drove her into town when she had to run errands. We hung out in my room and listened to music sometimes. She liked classic rock. I pretended I did. When I moved off campus I thought she would come over and we could take walks on the beach and stuff, you know? That probably sounds stupid."

"No," Grace says. "It sounds really nice."

"I just—" Charles's voice cracks. "I thought that she could like me too."

# # #

"Grace, we're playing tennis at four," her mother says as

Grace arrives back from a walk in the woods.

"Uh, no thanks," she says.

"Yes," her mother says, looking squarely at her.

"What? No. I'm not playing," Grace says, shaking her head.

"Yes you are. And that's final."

Grace realizes that tennis may be her mother's version of a duel. Her mother hands her a plate with a tuna sandwich on whole wheat.

"I don't play tennis anymore," Grace says.

"Then you'll be a little rusty. Lemonade?"

She eyes her mother above her sandwich as she takes a bite.

"Yes, please," she says.

"I have a racket you can use. And sneakers."

Her mother sets a big glass of iced lemonade in front of her.

"It would be good for you to run around. Get a little sun." She slides a napkin to Grace and sits across from her at the table. "You used to be such a good player."

"I was totally mediocre."

Her mother refuses the bait.

"Mom, I'm leaving tomorrow. My flight's in the morning."

Her mother closes her eyes and sighs.

"I figured this was coming. Considering your performance at the Chenowiths'."

"My performance? What about Dad's?"

"Grace. What are you so angry about? You're a grown woman. No, wait," she says, holding up her hand as Grace opens her mouth. "Frankly, I don't want to know. I don't care. I'm too old for this."

"I think it's fair to say it's not helping. Me being here."

"I don't get it with you two," her mother says, exasperated.

"Let's face it," Grace says breezily. "He thinks the wrong sister died."

Her mother's hand catches the edge of Grace's cheek, for the first time in her life, in an awkward slap. It feels hot and good.

"Goddamn you, Grace," she says. "You are infuriating." She straightens her headband and takes a deep breath through her nose. "I'm sorry. That was inexcusable."

"It's okay," Grace says. "It puts me in a better mood to beat you."

Her mother laughs a little. In her tired face, resting in the cradle of her palms, Grace sees her own.

"It doesn't matter what I say, does it? When did it stop mattering what I say?" her mother asks.

"Mom, there's no need for you to worry about me."

"I hope you know someday what it is to be a mother," she says.

"Don't hold your breath."

For a fleeting moment, her mom is the young woman

dressed in black in a church pew, sitting behind her husband, awash in loss. But then it's gone and she's up, whisking Grace's plate away to the dishwasher.

"Are you happy with your life?" her mother asks, looking out on the yard through the window above the sink.

"Are you?" Grace launches back.

Her mother swings around.

"What does that mean?"

Grace shrugs.

"What is it with you?" her mother asks. "Is that some sort of jab?"

"Forget it."

"No, Grace Elaine, I will not forget it. Do you disapprove of me, is that it?"

They stare, in standoff. Grace's face prickles in shame. She wishes her mother would slap her again and again. She wishes her mother would scream and throw things and tear her hair out.

"I made my choices and I'm content with them," her mother says. "Don't blame me if you're not so sure of your own."

"Sorry," Grace says, sliding down into her chair, regretting her childishness, weary of her provocation.

Her mother sits again at the table but looks out the window at a hummingbird hovering at the feeder.

"I know I wasn't the type of mother that put notes in

your lunchbox. Maybe I didn't hug you enough or ask about your feelings like they do these days."

"Mom."

"You seemed like you could take care of yourself. Better than the rest of us, anyway. Remember that time I forgot to pick you up from dance class? You must have been seven or eight. You walked home by yourself and never even got mad about it."

"I was mad," Grace says.

"You didn't say anything."

"Maybe I learned from the best."

Her mother presses her lips together.

"Karen says our daughters resent us because they have too many choices now. They wish they had the built-in excuse of a traditional role," she says.

"This coming from a woman who followed her husband to France when he ran away with another woman, begging him to take her back," Grace says.

"She didn't beg him. She knew what she wanted."

"Oh please," Grace says. "I suppose the facelift was for her, too."

"Cynicism does not become you," her mother says, standing and brushing crumbs from the table into her hand.

"What would become me? Fake cheer? A husband?"

Her mother shakes her head and empties the crumbs into the sink.

"We're leaving for the club in an hour," she says, as she walks out of the kitchen.

After Callie died, her mother spent days in her room, emerging occasionally when friends came by, her face tight, her eyes remote. She sipped at tea but that was the extent of her intake. Grace lurked just out of view, listening to the murmurs, the tinkling of spoons against china cups, feeling such enormous weight from above and pull from below that she thought if she gave in to it, she'd be sucked down into the center of the earth.

Her father shuffled between the bedroom and his closed office. He never looked at her.

※ ※ ※

They drive onto the meticulous grounds of the country club, canopied under the branches of 300-year-old oaks. Grace has avoided the club ever since college, appalled by the discrimination and the tacit approval of her parents and their friends. As a kid she didn't notice that everyone was white and Protestant, but she was acutely aware that in their town, one's family was either in or out, and when a club application was turned down, it was the subject of dinner-party whispering.

The grand old clubhouse is still impressive from the outside, colonial white with black shutters, but inside it is faded around the edges; the carpeting needs to be replaced, the gaudy chandeliers in the dining room are dated, and the old fox hunting–themed cocktail lodge is losing its luster. But out in back, where the manse spreads out into acres of verdant growth, the club is the same, stately with the ramshackle elegance of old money. The air is cool and frenzied birds call from leafy overhangs. From the wide balcony of the stone patio the first tee is visible below.

Grace hates that even now she feels the lulling familiarity of this place. She thinks of Charles reading a book of quotations in his cell, the walls the same color as the ceiling, in the greenish tinge of a single overhead lightbulb.

They walk down to the tennis area, where an aging pro with dyed-brown hair air-kisses her mother hello. Grace avoids an introduction and takes to the court.

She wears a faded black T-shirt and cut-off jeans, clothes she found in a giveaway pile in the garage. Her mother is in a sporty, navy and white striped tennis dress, legs toned and tan, and she is quick around the court. Grace drags her heavy, clunky feet, her chest tight after every point. She has to lean over to catch her breath. She misses every first serve and has to dink in a second. She hits wildly, going for winners and missing, unable to get her torpid body to the ball on time.

They play two sets. Her mother gleams, trouncing her 6-2, 6-1.

"I guess that settles it," her mother says, toweling off

her brow.

Grace sucks down water but it doesn't help.

# # #

"It's not like I didn't want to have friends," Charles says. "I just didn't know how other people did it."

"Friends are overrated," Grace says. "You know my only friend is my bartender back in Brooklyn?"

He laughs a little.

"I managed to shed everyone else."

"How come?" he asks.

"I prefer to be alone. I feel safer keeping things to myself."

"You're funny," he says.

"I'm going back to New York tomorrow. You can call me there," she says.

"Okay."

"I'll visit you."

He sighs.

"I'd like that, but unfortunately I'm only allowed three visits a week. And those are taken up by doctors and lawyers working on my defense."

"Oh. Maybe sometime soon, then," she says, trying to disguise her disappointment.

"You know, Sarah was so pretty and I'm not even sure she knew it. When she smiled it was like, pow!"

It's the most animated he's ever sounded.

"When I first saw her she was walking with two girls

who I kind of knew from the fraternity house. It was like they were in black and white, and only Sarah was in color. I waited for her after class so I could introduce myself. I felt okay about the whole thing, not like I was putting on an act or anything. She came to one of the happy hours in my room. Other guys talked to her and stuff but she talked to me, too. She listened. She was cool. And she didn't even have to try."

He stops talking.

"What else?" she asks.

He pauses, tired out by his remembrance.

"Her favorite album was *Blood on the Tracks* by Bob Dylan. It wasn't my type but I grew to like it because she did. I used to drive her to yoga class and wait for her, then drive her back to campus. I don't know. We were friends."

Her mother calls her down to dinner and Grace is not quick enough to cover the mouthpiece of the phone.

"You're so lucky," he says.

"Sorry," she says.

"It's okay," he says.

"There's something I wanted to tell you," Grace says. "An image you might think about when it starts to get dark. This morning when I woke up, I saw spring tree leaves of a million shades of green from the window. A clear pale sky. And each time the wind blew, there was a flutter of pink petals from a crabapple tree."

"Wow," he says. "Nice."

# # #

In the morning, when it's time to leave for the airport, Grace finds her dad in his office where he has spent the night in his chair, slouched down, his head cocked to the side, mouth open as if mid-gasp. A dribble of pesto from dinner dots the front of his shirt just below his chin. His once-chiseled face hangs under white stubble. A half-empty bottle rests beside him, the picture of the four of them hand in hand crookedly replaced on the wall.

She straightens the frame but doesn't wake him to say goodbye.

———

Investigators are still trying to determine if sexual contact occurred after the Shafer killing, which would be characteristic of a sadomasochistic sadosexual murder. Still, they acknowledge that some questions may never be answered.

———

## CHAPTER 23

After the disorienting third-world quality of JFK, Grace pushes her way outside the airport only to be greeted by the onset of a terrible New York summer. It's like walking into a billow of noxious steam. The air–conditioning is out in the cab she gets, and the maniacal maneuvering of its driver, jerking stop-and-go through potholed narrow lanes, leaves her ready to throw up in her purse.

Her apartment is a baked, stale tomb, blandly without character. After nine years, it looks like she's here only temporarily. There are three messages: one from her mother, checking that she made it back, one from Brian confirming her appearance at the office tomorrow, and one wrong-number fax that beeps for ten minutes. When she opens the window, the faintly sweet odor of decaying garbage with a hint of urine drifts in.

She stuffs a twenty and her keys in her pocket.

Inside the heavy door of Chances, it's cool and dark, with blues playing low. Jimmy leans against the bar with a towel in hand, watching a Mets game on the television in the corner. After a strikeout he turns and grins wide when he sees her.

"Well, well," he says.

"Hello there."

"Did you miss me?"

"Always," she says.

He sets a wine glass in front of her usual seat. She has a flash of sad recognition when she sees herself in the mirror behind the bar, a woman who drinks too much and who is most comfortable here. But her first sip wipes it away.

"Good to have you back," he says. "How's things?"

"Okay. I had to go home for a while. My dad had a stroke."

"Oh, I'm so sorry to hear that. You look a little tired, Gracie."

"I am," she says, drinking down the wine.

"I was thinking about you the other day. I heard they might go for the death penalty for that kid who killed the girl."

"Yeah," she says.

"Do you still think he's innocent?"

"Who is, Jimmy?"

"Touché," he says.

Grace doesn't have the energy to explain. She wants to put her head against the smooth oak of the bar and sleep.

A rowdy group of post-softball-game men bursts in from the bright outside, commandeering some tables and dropping their gear. One of them, red-faced and sweaty with a pointed nose and big teeth, approaches the bar, shouting a pitcher order. He smiles at her but she turns away.

She slips out as Jimmy busies himself with the tap.

# # #

It's as if Grace has been gone from the office for months and everything shifted in her absence—the flecked gray carpeting is new, as are the two girls who titter by in short skirts, and the copier has been moved. The horrible fluorescent lighting is harsh and revealing, leaving nowhere for her to blend in unnoticed. Her heart beats like a jackrabbit's, like she is all of a sudden the only non-alien in a sci-fi movie, in danger of being discovered. Anxiety pools in her chest. She sucks in mammoth breaths to try to quell her panic.

But then she sees the familiar bounce of Brian's mop-top head and she knows she is cornered.

"Grace!" he says as he rounds the padded wall.

He has a new look going, with cowboy boots and a large trucker belt buckle, an outfit he has surely trotted out for her return.

"Hi, Brian," she says.

She half-stands to meet his hug, then quickly disengages.

"Welcome back. I'll let you get settled in."

He snaps his fingers to punctuate his exit.

"Hey, Grace?" he says, turning back.

"Yeah?"

"Do you have plans tonight? I was thinking we could grab a drink?"

She wants to be away from here and alone. She wants to be numb.

"Yeah, okay," she says.

He waves and walks away.

There is a layer of dust on her computer screen; she wipes it off with a tissue. She picks up a stack of layouts from her inbox and sets them on the desk in front of her. The small printed letters blur. She reads and rereads the headlines but can't get beyond them. She abandons the pages and opens up her email, only to find 236 messages: meetings, announcements, jokes, birthdays, goodbyes from people she never knew, 401(k) updates, IT server warnings, emergency-preparedness guidelines. She deletes them all.

Online she finds the same news bits on Charles she has already pored over. She hears the drone of the lights overhead, the lite FM from another cube, the loud adsales guy on his speakerphone down the hall.

What if the key to the story lies with Sarah? Was she just pretty and fun and nice? Grace remembers Amy, the girl from the dorm. She was trying to fit in, too. Though more successful at it than Charles, she was still watchful, hungry, monitoring everyone else around her for cues about when to laugh, what to say, how to look, who to know. She would have observed everything she could have about a girl everyone liked.

An email arrives from Brian about a status meeting. Grace can't will herself to click it open. *How can I care*, she thinks, *when a person's life is at stake?* She feels frazzled, sick, eroded.

She grabs her bag and makes a run for it. Outside, she catches a cab to Grand Central and finds a Long Island Railroad train heading out to Emeryville.

⚓ ⚓ ⚓

Grace goes straight to Charles's dorm but finds the door locked and no one milling about. Campus is quiet. A kid walks through the breezeway carrying a plastic tub with a basketball, a comforter, and a fan inside. He's in Birkenstocks and cargo shorts, his hair grown out and chlorine-tinged at its ends.

"Hi," she says. "Can you help me? I'm looking for Amy. Amy Monroe."

He bobbles the box and hikes it up on his hip.

"Yeah, I don't know. I haven't seen her. I think she

lives in there?"

He motions with his head to the dorm and walks toward the parking lot.

In the phone booth out front, Grace gets Amy's number from the campus operator and dials.

"Hello?"

"Hi. Amy? This is the woman who you talked to a few weeks ago. About Charles Raggatt."

"Look, I don't know how you got this number, but…"

"I just wanted to speak with you. For a minute."

"I don't think so. Listen, please don't call me again."

"It's important. For Charles."

Amy hangs up. Grace sits on the bench and waits.

An hour later, Amy exits the door of the building, grappling with a pile of books. Her red roots are showing more and she looks younger without makeup.

"Hello," Grace says, standing.

Amy looks up and squints a little, then quickly looks to see if anyone else is around.

"Please, I told you," she says.

But in her weak refusal Grace sees her way in. Amy starts walking and Grace moves in step next to her.

"I can't talk to you about that stuff," Amy says.

"Can I help you with those?"

"I'm fine."

Amy's arms strain, her white knuckles gripping the

bottom of the stack.

"I don't want to talk about Charles," Grace says.

Amy glances at Grace through her hair.

"I wondered if you knew Sarah."

Amy tries to straighten up and a book falls off. Grace picks it up and then Amy lets her take some of the textbooks.

"I need to go sell these back."

She points with her shoulder toward the bookstore.

"Anything you remember about her," Grace says.

Amy blows hair from her eye.

"Sarah was great. Everybody liked her."

"Were you friends with her?"

"I mean, we weren't super-close or anything, but whatever. We were in the same yoga class."

A bell chimes for noon as they walk past a clock tower.

"It sounds like she had everything going for her," Grace says.

"Yeah, I guess. I think it's kind of weird that they painted such a spotless picture of her, you know? No one's that perfect," Amy says.

She looks behind and wipes her cheek with her shoulder.

"How so?" Grace asks.

"I don't know. She was a total partyer, for one." She lowers her voice. "She did a lot of drugs. It wasn't that big of a secret."

Amy makes an exaggerated sniff noise.

"Cocaine?"

"By the spring she'd gotten super-skinny."

They pass a guy in an Emeryville Swimming sweat-shirt.

"Hey, Amy," he says without stopping.

"Hey, Doug," she says with a fake smile.

A few steps later Amy stops.

"I know it's not cool of me to say bad stuff about a dead person. But it's not like she was a saint." She bites a piece of skin on her lip and frowns, then resumes walking. "I saw him give her money once."

"Who?"

Grace's stomach hardens.

"Charles. I saw him give Sarah money."

"What? Money for what?"

"I don't know. I just saw it, okay? He gave her a bunch of twenties when he didn't know I was looking."

Drugs. Money. The revelations cast a crooked light, and doubt edges its way into the periphery of Grace's conviction.

"You have to tell me everything you know," Grace says. "What were they involved in?"

"That's it. That's all I know," Amy says. "I shouldn't have even said that. Listen, I have to go. I can take these from here."

Grace stacks her books on top of Amy's. Amy walks

away, stooped under the weight, her shoulders rounded, her eyes on the ground.

On the train back into the city Grace slumps into a window seat and rests her head against the glass. She sees Charles's face when she closes her eyes. When she opens them she thinks, for the first time, *What if I have been wrong?*

## CHAPTER 24

They are in your rearview mirror, your parents and your sister, small and framed, watching you drive away. This is how you will remember them, miniature, your mother with her coral-colored lips—you imagine she gives a beauty pageant wave—and your father, relieved, already starting to walk back inside, checking you off his list. Caroline is waving like crazy, her bright face filled up by her smile, by white teeth. You could squeeze them all between your thumb and forefinger. Glorious, so glorious is this moment that a tear leaks out of your eye. Who the new you will be is almost too much to take. You are free to try again, to become someone else. It's going to be the turning point. The next time you come back to Hunter, it will be triumphant.

It's late by the time you arrive at Emeryville College and find *your dorm. The high that has kept you company across Ohio, Pennsylvania, New Jersey, and New York teeters a little when you step out of your car into the dark parking lot and a group of attractive students walks by, laughing and talking on their way to a party. You smile at them but only after they have already passed by.*

You are a little disappointed that there is no welcome table set up, not even a banner above the door, but you tell yourself it's okay, you're okay. In the lobby there is a map on the wall with photos of incoming students and where each is from. There's you but it's not the you that you imagined on the drive out. Your face is puffy, filling up the little square, your smile forced, your hair too gelled. It was your senior picture and your mom must have sent it in. The other kids look pretty and handsome and happy. You hear someone playing guitar down the hall and then the tinkle of a girl's laughter. From upstairs you hear people talking in the way that you could never do. Just talking. Has everyone already made friends? Did you get here on the wrong day? Breathe.

When you get upstairs where your room is, kids are hanging out in the hall, in doorways, in groups and pairs.

"Hey, what's up, guys?" you say with gusto, putting your hand up for high fives.

You see them calculate who you are: the outgoing fun guy, the party man. Soon you'll be the rich kid whose stuff is nicer than everyone else's. So far, so good, you think. I can do this.

"Hey, man," you say to a preppy kid in a Milton Lacrosse shirt. "Charles Raggatt."

You put out your hand. He shakes it with a little laugh. "Hey. Josh Peterson."

As you turn away, you see him exchange a look with a lanky, blond swimmer type. You know in your gut that the look is about you, that they are not fooled. Already they have figured you out. It's not possible, you think. It can't be. You shove the thought down and decide you will do anything in your power to win them over.

After you have brought everything in from your car— no one offers to help—you go about setting up your TV and stereo, pretending to be cool about it, but testing the volume too loudly so people will notice. Your roommate, John Kim, seems pretty nice, if a little reserved and unimpressed by all your gear. Maybe you'll be friends, but he's not quite what you'd envisioned.

You step out into the hall and announce, "Party Saturday night. Room 24. The keg is going to flow."

A couple girls cheer but then go back to their conversation.

"Dude, do you have a car?" Josh Peterson asks.

"Yep," you say.

"Think you could help us out tomorrow? We have to get a broken pool table to the dump."

Josh, it turns out, is already an SAE, the best fraternity on campus. He came early to rush. You didn't know anything about it.

"*Totally. Just grab me whenever,*" *you say, thinking this may be your ticket in.*

"*All right,*" *he says.*

You go back in your room and sit on your bare mattress, overwhelmed, unsure of what to do. Your roommate plays Tetris on his computer. Your head feels like an overloaded circuit board. You feel dislocated from your body.

"*I'm going to go grab some food,*" *you say to the back of his head.* "*Want anything?*"

"*No, thanks,*" *he says, tapping the keys to steer his piece on–screen.* "*Damn,*" *he says when the game ends, and turns to you as you pretend to look for your keys.* "*I'll probably go to bed soon, if that's okay with you?*"

"*Yeah, totally. Sorry I got here so late. I'll unpack to-morrow.*"

You spread your sheets haphazardly on your bed and step over stereo components to get to the door.

"*Oh, Charles,*" *he says,* "*some of us are going out tomor-row for pizza. If you want to come?*"

"*Yeah, okay,*" *you say, thankful to be included for once, and yet so confused about who you're supposed to be.*

The hall crowd has thinned.

"*Hey, anyone want anything? I'm making a food run,*" *you say.*

Shaking of heads and "*no, thanks*" *and you go out alone, willing yourself not to start running to try to ditch your skin, to tear it off and leave it in a heap in the dirt.*

#

You go to your classes but you barely do the work. You're too busy planning nightly happy hour in your room, stocking it with mixers and snacks, bottles of booze. (You're never even asked for your ID on account of your size and your gold card.) The best part is, everyone comes by. People from the dorm and people you've never seen before. They slap you on the back and yell "Raggatt" in salute and you can barely believe it. You finally have a glimpse of the glow of popularity that has always eluded you. So what if they come for the free drinks? You'll take it. You're pretty sure you're becoming "that guy" and that's what matters. Girls even treat you differently now. They talk to you and let you drive them places. Amy with the strawberry hair laughs at your jokes even if she isn't interested in going out with you.

And the SAEs, they like you. You drive them places and buy kegs for them and hang out. When you're drunk you dance to make them laugh. You buy them a foosball table and a pinball machine. They tell you that you are their mascot.

When the year goes on and people stop coming by and you stop getting invited places and the SAEs stop calling except when they need something and even John Kim stops living in your room when he gets a girlfriend, you think that you cannot stop or you will die. Drink more. Buy more. Eat more. Be used more. You patch the fissures and holes with anything you can find. You take sleeping pills to lose yourself *for fifteen hours at a time. You find refuge at the donut shop with the nice woman who treats you like you're human. You watch porn instead of going to class. You drive into New York City looking for prostitutes but you can't even figure out where to go. When you do find a drugged-out woman on Eleventh Avenue she demands you give her $200 and then walks away when you hand over your cash. You sit in your car and eat KFC and cry and think about how it all went so very wrong. Again.*

And then you see her and you can't believe you've been at school for weeks and not seen her before. Dark eyes, light hair, a lopsided smile, an electricity about her that sends a zing down to your toes, and even as you know that she could not possibly ever like you, her existence is a reason to keep it all together.

You put your faith in Sarah Shafer.

## CHAPTER 25

Grace calls Brian from the station, blaming her afternoon disappearance on a forgotten series of doctors' appointments, and he has her meet him at an East Village dive down the street from the one where she humiliated herself last time. She just wants to feel dulled, blotted out, and at the moment she doesn't even care that Brian will be sitting next to her.

She orders two vodka tonics and then asks Brian, who is getting situated and finally hooks his boot heels on the rung of the stool, what he wants. He laughs, thinking she's joking.

"Oh. I guess I'll have a bourbon then," he says, quickly covering his shock at her double drink order.

The bartender wears eyeliner and black nail polish, and he mouths along to the music as he pours the drinks.

"To your return," Brian says, trying to sound casual.

He lifts his glass in her direction.

She breathes in the warm, sweet oak scent of his bourbon, with all its memory-soaked associations, then downs her first drink in four long gulps.

A couple of weeks after Callie's funeral, Grace's mother went to Chicago to stay with her own mother. One night Grace awoke to voices, loud whispers, and stifled laughs coming from downstairs. Her first panicked thought was that it was burglars, so she crept to her parents' bedroom. The bed was empty. From the banister she peered down, like she and Callie had done during parties, and saw a sliver of light coming from the study.

"Shhhh. You must be very, very quiet," her dad said in an Elmer Fudd voice.

A woman snorted. The smell of cigarettes sneaked out from under the door. Someone knocked into a lamp.

Grace made her way downstairs and slid along the wall to the living room and to the bar. There were two glasses, one with red lipstick—what her mother would have called *a floozy shade*—and a quarter-bottle of Maker's Mark. And then she found a red silk scarf on the floor and she knew it was some kind of sign meant for her. She knew it was her fault, that without Callie, her parents' tie to each other was unraveling, that this woman was here because of what Grace had done. It was all part of her punishment. She put the bottle to her nose, breathing it so deep her eyes watered. And then she drank. But the burning fury in her throat made her gag and spit it out onto her posy-print nightgown.

Brian tilts his head in a question and a look passes over his face, a quick tightening of his eyes.

"You should know I'm really pretty dull," Grace says, in the depths of her second drink.

"What?" he asks.

"Nothing," she says.

"I see you forgot to wind your watch again," he says pointing to her wrist.

"I guess I don't ever care enough what time it is," she says.

He smiles.

"You're really not like other people, Grace."

She laughs.

"I missed you," he says to his lap.

Grace sits up quickly, spilling her purse. She bends down for its contents on the floor, hiding for a moment behind her hair as she stuffs her wallet and keys back inside.

"I mean I missed having you around. At the office. That place," he shakes his head with wide eyes. "It's kind of the nut house."

She wants to slither to the floor and snake her way out.

"Yeah," she says. "Well."

"So," he says. "How are you?"

She laughs.

"I'm okay. You?"

Grace tunes out while he talks about work. Instead she thinks of Charles, his hope depleted, then refilled, again and again. She sees him waiting for Sarah outside her yoga class, checking himself in the mirror, chewing mints, practicing what he'd say to her when she got back in the car.

Brian has asked her something that she has missed. His brow scrunches.

"What?" she asks.

"You don't think I'm like that, do you?" he asks.

"No, of course not," Grace says, ordering another round. She feels like she is watching from three feet away. "Sorry," she says, touching his arm, "I've just had a lot on my mind. My dad getting sick and all that."

He presses his lips together and nods, then takes her cold hand and interlaces his fingers with hers.

"Oh," she says, and smiles despite herself.

They drink and drink—or at least Grace does—and then she slurs, "Let's go to your place," because she can't stand the uncomfortable waters he is trying to navigate in telling her he likes her, because sleeping with him would be easier than talking.

Brian looks a little frightened by the whole thing but

his libido gets the best of him and he leads her blundering down Avenue C. Inside the building, he says it's just four flights up and she collapses on the dirty bottom step.

"Do you want me to carry you?" he asks.

"God, no," she says, rolling over and crawling up on all fours.

Brian looks stricken.

"Grace," he says, once inside the apartment. He pushes her shoulders back against the door. "Look at me."

His face is lit from the streetlight through the window.

"This is serious for me," he says, his bourbon breath a powerful elixir. She halfheartedly bats his arm away but he grips her harder. "I want to get to know you," he says insistently. "What's going on in there?"

She feels the salty burn of tears just under the surface and she fears if she lets them begin, they won't stop, and they will drench her, then flood the apartment, then wash out the whole city.

"Hey," she manages to say. "It's just me."

And she kisses him, aiming for his mouth but getting only part of a lip. There is awkward fumbling with buttons and zippers in the dark. She goes at it feverishly —anything to avoid words. She loses herself to his body and his warmth.

When Grace wakes up, disoriented and still slightly drunk, there is Brian, lying next to her in a fetal position, her watch around his wrist. His sheets smell like baby shampoo.

She finds the rest of her clothes and slips out into the hall to dress.

The predawn night is warm and quiet and, as she passes the park, the birds' manic chittering announces the coming of day. There is only the occasional car, certainly no cabs, so she walks toward home, unafraid of who might be lurking about. She is invisible.

# # #

Brian calls five times and leaves two messages. Grace lies in bed and hides, and from her window watches dark-skinned nannies push white babies up the sidewalk. The super and his wife sit on the front stoop and chatter on all through the day, a lulling Spanish backdrop. It is summer and the city has a fullness to it, swollen with heat and moisture, and ripe with rot. Her ineffectual air conditioner rattles on. After getting the mail, she is back inside her room with a throbbing head that feels like it's threatening to burst.

# # #

"I'm so glad you're there," Charles says.

"How have you been the past few days?" Grace asks.

She is wary of him now, tired of not knowing enough.

"I've been better. I mean, not that I've been feeling better but I've had better days than these. Sorry," he says.

"They've found me competent to stand trial. But my lawyer is sticking to his strategy. He calls it mental duress."

"Sometimes I think you want to go to jail forever," she says flatly.

"I know, it's just—"

"I know about the drugs," she says.

"What?" he asks.

"I know Sarah had a cocaine problem."

"Who told you that? It's not true."

"It doesn't matter who told me. It *is* true."

He doesn't answer and she waits.

"You can't tell anybody that."

"It's the truth, right?"

"She had some trouble. But she's gone now. It doesn't matter." His voice falters.

"Tell me about the money, then," she says.

"Oh," he groans.

"Why did you give her money?"

"There's a saying I found in the quotation book. 'Dripping water hollows a stone.'"

"Goddamnit, Charles," she says.

He is quiet. She sets her jaw and twists a section of her hair.

"No one was supposed to know about it. I was so happy to help her the first time she asked," he says. "She said she was running short for the month and needed to buy some books. I gave her $100. I said that she didn't have to pay me back. I got a big allowance so it wasn't that big a deal."

"And then she asked you for more?"

"It started happening pretty regularly."

"Didn't you feel like she was using you?"

"Whenever I would feel insecure about it, there she would be, this beautiful person sitting on my couch. I told her about how I had always been a loser and she would tell me it wasn't true. She told me I was generous and fun and smart." A sad and disillusioned laugh leaks out. "When I was with her, I believed her."

"I'm sorry," Grace says.

"We didn't hang out together at parties or anything but that was okay. I didn't care that she dated around. It took me a while to figure out the money was going for drugs. I don't think anyone really knew the extent of it. But even when I knew, I couldn't say no. I wanted to help but she didn't want to hear it from me."

He sighs heavily.

"I miss her laugh," he says. "She had a kind of tomboy laugh that you knew wasn't fake. I feel bad that I told you about that money stuff. It's not fair to talk about now."

"I need to know these things."

He doesn't respond, the silence extending.

"Do know what a rock polisher is?" she asks finally.

"No, I don't think so."

"You must be too young. It was a fad in the seventies.

It was this little machine where you dropped in a regular stone and, after a crazy racket, it would come out a smooth and shiny nugget."

"That's kind of cool," he says. "I probably would have liked something like that when I was young."

"My dad gave me one for my tenth birthday. I was so excited, not just to have it but because it was something we could do together," she says. "But of course it was never the right time. And then one night when I got home from my tennis lesson, I heard the telltale grinding sound from the basement. I walked down the stairs and there they were, my dad and Callie, amazing themselves with their creations."

"That sucks," he says. "What did you do?"

"Nothing. His back was to me so he didn't know I was there. But she did. She glanced at me with a smug smile and then went back to the project at hand."

Grace remembers the anger, cold and inward. When she imagines herself she sees only dark hair and a blurry face. But she can always conjure up Callie.

———

Nassau County prosecutors will seek the death penalty for Charles Raggatt, the wealthy Emeryville College student charged with killing classmate Sarah Shafer, a well-liked communications major.

Prosecutors believe Raggatt—who threw lavish parties—drugged Shafer, then lured her to a motel room where he held her against her will and made sexual advances, which she rebuffed. He then stabbed her in a rage. After the killing, he wrapped the body in plastic bags and kept it in his car before burying it in a shallow grave behind his rented beach condo.

"This was a vicious, brutal, premeditated murder. A horrendous homicide," said John Cavanaugh, who heads the District Attorney's Major Offense Bureau.

———

## CHAPTER 26

By midafternoon, Grace has hives dotted across her shoulders, chest, and neck—insistent and itchy welts that she has scratched raw.

It's so hot it's quiet outside, the sounds absorbed by the shimmering asphalt and wilting trees, the air thick and hazy. Strollered children have damp faces, their hairlines moist. The roasting sidewalk makes Grace's flip-flops stick and she can't open her eyes all the way, like she has stepped into a familiar anxiety dream. She gives in to the languid steaminess, moving slowly, trancelike, downhill past the rotting vomit smell of the garbage bins outside of McDonald's and the crisp, taunting air-conditioned breaths from open shop doors.

The liquor store has fifths of vodka in the back freezer. She buys one, and, holding the cold paper bag next to her belly, searches for her car, which she hasn't used in weeks. After some futile wanderings, she finds it parked in front of a razor wire–fenced empty lot, a back window broken out, a transient's beer cans and trash in the front seat, a stack of orange, weather-beaten parking tickets under the windshield wiper. She brushes them off onto the street like dead leaves and slides into the baking driver's seat. The heat makes her shiver.

She's supposed to be at work but she has blocked it out. The vodka is cheap but its harshness is blunted by a forgiving chill. Between swallows she holds the wet, cold bottle against the hives on her chest. The air conditioner labors, overmatched. In the rearview mirror the circles under her eyes are ashy moons, her cheekbones are severe ledges, and the hives on her neck have fused into one big inflamed bump over her collarbone. She flips the mirror to the ceiling.

Grace drives fast out of Brooklyn and Queens, flying east on the Long Island Expressway back to Emeryville. By the time she reaches fraternity row she is riled up, primed for confrontation. A painter has worked halfway across the top floor of the SAE house and there is only a solitary mountain bike outside. She bangs on the front door with the side of her fist. No one answers. She tries kicking.

A young, bespectacled guy in basketball shorts answers the door.

"Can I help you?"

His tousled hair suggests he has just woken up and this makes Grace even angrier. She thrusts her face at his.

"Did you know Charles Raggatt?" she demands.

"That murderer kid?"

"The one you and your frat buddies toyed with and sponged off of," she spits, pointing her finger at his chest.

"Whoa, lady. I'm just living here for summer school. I didn't know the guy. I don't even go here."

"Oh," she says, sinking into herself, disoriented. "Sorry." She takes a step back; he must think she is deranged. "I'm just upset."

"Yeah, okay," he says, closing the door some.

He flicks his eyes past her, and she knows he's about to call campus police.

She scurries back to the car, takes a nip from the bottle, and drives straight to town. She goes to the donut shop, but a girl with pink pigtails is behind the counter. The teamster is not at the diner, where Grace sits for two minutes with a Coke. She is a hamster on a wheel, after something, anything, around and around.

She drives out toward the beach, to the nondescript stucco complex called The Landings where Charles felt his mind slip through his hands, and where he buried Sarah Shafer's body behind the barbecue pit. There are two buildings of eight units each; Charles lived on the very end. Easy anonymity with nice amenities. It could be anywhere. Although the place lacks character, it has a walkway to the beach, which would have appealed to his need to show off in the only way he knew how. In interviews with police, none of the residents claimed to have known him. His upstairs neighbor said only that he had been exceedingly polite and had kept to himself.

Grace parks in one of the reserved spaces. Closed blinds block the windows of the apartment where Charles lived, so she slips behind the building. And there it is, the patio with picnic tables and a brick grill. At the edge, a large discolored patch of sandy earth. No one ever noticed anything. He must have been so quiet and neat when he buried her body. What did he think when he was done? Could he push the feel of her cold skin from his mind? Could he ever really rid himself of the stench of her?

Knowing Charles, she thinks, *he called the police on himself.* He led them straight to him because he could think of no other way, no one else to become.

It is cooler out here with the ocean breeze. Grace returns to the car for her depleted bottle and then follows the path toward the water, sliding off her shoes. There are a few people scattered about, but because it's a weekday, the beach is relatively empty. The sand burns coarse and hot on her soles, and she walks quickly to the water's edge where small waves lap the shore. She wades in, soaking her gypsy skirt up to her knees.

She hasn't been in the ocean since she was sixteen, the

last vacation she took with her parents. They went every summer for two weeks with other families from the circuit to the Outer Banks of North Carolina. They all rented big houses and evenings were spent drinking on alternate verandahs. The kids she'd grown up with went jet skiing and surfing and drank beer around bonfires at night. Grace was sullen and sat in the sun by herself or stayed inside, getting high and reading cheap mysteries. She wanted to be gone; she couldn't wait for college.

On the last day, when everyone else went on an outing to the giant sand dunes, she sat on the beach in her bikini, feeling the sun burn her skin and wishing it would scorch her into ash. But something drew her to the ocean that afternoon and she walked straight in, as if mesmerized, dunked repeatedly by large breakers until she could get past them, oblivious to the warning flag flying from the lifeguard perch just down the beach, not noticing that no one else was in the water. She could feel the pull underneath but it wasn't until she was far enough out and could no longer stand that the rip current snatched hold of her and pulled her along. She watched the mainland with wonder as she was carried down the shore and out further into the ocean. It was such a delicious letting go. She was giddy, almost euphoric. *I will go this way*, she said to herself, *and it will be fine*. She thought about how she would see Callie again and how she might explain everything. She imagined her parents at her funeral, sitting together this time. But then she was tugged downward, pulled under the water, and panic set in, her body reacting with primal urgency to survive. She kicked and flailed, struggling to extricate herself, gasping. She fought. And then all at once, she was spit out in some convergence of currents. When she grappled her way back to the shore she was a mile and a half down the beach.

The salt water burns her lacerated hives. She welcomes it. She walks further out, all the way into the water, her too-large tank top floating around her body and her skirt weighing her down. As she treads water she can see the roof of The Landings. Her brain is calm and fuzzy, and she angles her face toward the sun.

"Hey!" a gray-haired man calls from the beach.

His khakis are rolled up, his button-down untucked. He carries a sketchbook and a small easel. She ignores him and tilts her face up.

"Hey, are you okay out there?"

Grace raises her hand and waves but he doesn't move. He sets down his things and walks into the shallow water.

"Are you in trouble?" he yells through his hands.

She's afraid he's about to jump in after her, so she swims until she can stand and tries to shoo him on. He plants his feet, his hands at his hips, waiting until she gets all the way out of the water.

"Not on my watch," he says.

She passes him without looking at his face and retrieves her bottle on the way back to the car.

The block of county buildings in Mineola is massive and imposing and barely navigable. Grace circles the courthouse twice and asks directions from a listless employee on a smoke break before she finds a sign pointing toward the jail. Once inside, the walls are a sickly yellow-tinged beige, hopelessly institutional. Brown plastic chairs are bolted to the scuffed linoleum floor.

Grace's wet clothes cling to her skin, her hair is half-dry and stringy, her breath flammable. After passing through a metal detector—a female security guard raises her eyes at Grace's appearance—she follows the posted arrows to an old wood-and-glass door that looks more like the entry to a principal's office than a jailhouse. Inside there is a high counter with a Plexiglas partition and a metal grate through which to talk. A few policemen wander about a series of desks, bantering and laughing. Their pace is easy and carefree, almost old-fashioned, until they see Grace knocking on the window. She is thankful for the wall between them. At least her hives, crusty from the salt water, have stopped itching so she's not clawing at her chest.

"I'm here to see a prisoner?" she says too loudly.

The young cop at the front, his biceps pumped up bigger than the rest of him, squints his eyes at her. He points to a wall with a list of visiting hours and protocol. She skips over the small type, unable to read the words, but at the end of the list, in all capitals, she's able to make out, NO EXCEPTIONS!

"Excuse me," she says into the speak-through.

He ambles back.

"Yeah?" he says into the microphone, a small smile curling the edges of his mouth.

The others toss bemused glances in her direction.

"It's extremely important. I'm with the press."

The lie slides off her drunken tongue.

The policeman must be bored enough pushing papers that his curiosity keeps him playing along. He sits and types something into the computer.

"Who are you trying to see, ma'am?"

"Charles Raggatt."

He licks his lips.

"Charles Raggatt. He's a special case," he says. "I'll check, but I don't think anyone's getting in there." His fingertips click the keyboard. "Nope. Closed for business."

"You don't understand," she says. "He would want to see me."

"I'm sure he'd want a lot of things," he says, and the older cop behind him suppresses a laugh. "I don't make the rules."

Her giant welt throbs.

"Please," she says, her palm against the partition.

He shakes his head, and then crosses his bulging arms. One of the policemen behind him twirls his finger next to his temple. Cuckoo.

"This is fucked," Grace says, slapping her hand against the plastic, leaving a smudged handprint.

"We're going to have to ask you to leave," the cop says with condescending measure, used to crazies wandering in.

"Officer," she says, trying to keep her voice low and steady.

"Sergeant," he says.

"Sorry. Sergeant. I work for a magazine."

His cocked head and squinting eyes say, "Sure, lady."

But she doesn't have anything to follow it up with. The man's face softens a bit when she falls silent.

"I'm sorry," she says quietly, backing away. "I'm very sorry."

Her flip-flops echo with each retreating step.

The sky is a muted pink as the parking lot empties out around her. She sits and watches the color seep out of the horizon from her windshield. When it's dark, she drives out to the backside of Hickton, to the Econo Lodge, and parks across the street in the weedy, cracked-asphalt parking lot of a shut-down trophy company. There are only three motel rooms lit, the sallow light outlining cheap polyester curtains. She drinks down the rest of the vodka without a breath.

Grace sees Charles's face in a dark window, searching for a reason not to kill himself, wondering if anyone would care if he did. She closes her eyes and tries to steady her spinning head. She is running out of time.

She puts her car in reverse, or she thinks she does. But when she jams on the accelerator, the car leaps forward and she is confused, wasted, and she spins the wheel and misses the brake and skids straight into a cement pylon. The edge of her right eye cracks against the steering wheel. And then it is quiet, with only the faraway sound of the highway and the ticking of her stalled engine. She opens the door and wobbles on quivering legs to the front of the car, where she sees through one eye that the fender is smashed and a headlight is broken out. There are no cars around and no one has seen her, but she can't risk the police. Her hands shake as she carefully adjusts the car into park and restarts the ignition.

"Some of the things that happened between Raggatt and the victim we may never be able to clarify to our satisfaction," said Lt. Jim Batrone. "There were only two people in that room."

## CHAPTER 27

Grace double-parks her damaged car in front of Brian's building. He buzzes her in.

When he opens the door, his face constricts in horror.

"Oh my God. Grace, what happened?" He moves aside to let her inside. His hand goes out to touch her shoulder but she moves away. "Are you okay?"

She catches herself in a small mirror that hangs by the door.

"Wow," she says.

Her eye is swollen and turning purple, her clothes are still damp, her skin streaked red from scratching. She is a wreck. She starts to giggle, then to laugh. Brian joins in but then he stops. She gathers herself and falls into a chair.

"I don't know why I came here," she says.

"What happened?"

"A little accident in the car," she says too glibly.

"Did you go to the doctor?"

"I'm fine," she says, waving him away.

Brian is bewildered. He goes to the kitchen searching for some ice and returns with a bag of frozen peas and a towel.

"Thanks," she says.

The cold stings her face.

"Grace," he says quietly. "I can't believe you drove like this."

"I can see out of my other," she says, pointing to her left eye.

"No, I mean lit. I can smell you from here." He leans forward with his hands on his knees. "I don't know what to say. You could have killed yourself. Jesus. Where have you been, anyway? I've been worried about you."

"None of that," she says.

And finally there is a spark of anger from him.

"You don't get to decide, Grace."

He stands and runs his hands through his hair, pacing before the window.

"People don't just not show up for work and run away after spending the night and drive drunk," he says.

"I'm sorry," she says, chewing on her thumbnail. "I've been doing something. Trying to help this kid."

"What are you talking about?"

"Out at Emeryville College. The boy they say killed

the girl."

"I don't get it," he says. "I thought they caught him and he confessed."

"They did. He did. But it doesn't make sense."

"It makes sense because he was a loser. A bad person," Brian says in a high voice, near hysterical. "What are you talking about?"

"I know him. We talk. I know it didn't happen like they say it did, like they'll prosecute him for. He's not some psychopath."

"So his lawyers can explain it for him."

"They won't! Because he doesn't want to save himself."

Brian is down on his knees in front of her.

"Stop, Grace. Stop it."

"I can't," she says. "It's too important."

He leans back on his heels and puts his face in his hands.

"Why don't you just come back to work and we can date like normal people? Why is that so bad? Why is being normal such a terrible thing?"

Her uncovered eye darts around the room.

"Why do you care about this guy so much? Why does it matter? He killed a girl, Grace."

Brian stands and goes back over to the couch.

"What's the worst thing you've ever done?" she asks.

"What?"

"You. What's the worst thing you've ever done?"

"Goddamnit, Grace," he says in a plaintive voice, "this isn't about me. This is crazy. Just stop."

"I'm serious," she says, dropping the peas into her lap.

He exhales, drained, his chin in his palm.

"What if that one thing, that one moment of darkness or selfishness was your definer?"

He shakes his head.

"It doesn't matter what came before it or after it, nothing will ever measure up. Nothing else will ever matter," she says. "That one second determines you. Forever."

"Okay," he says, "so it's not fair. But it happens all the time. That's the way the world works." He is spent. She wonders if it is enough to make him let her go. "Walk away, Grace. You need to pull yourself together."

Brian runs her a hot shower and hands her a T-shirt and boxers. He tucks her in on the couch. She sleeps like a stone, then wakes sometime in the night. Miraculously her car has not been towed, and there it waits, its hazard lights the heartbeat of a battered body.

# # #

"How are you?" Grace asks.

"My mood is pretty dark, I guess. I'm not sleeping very well. My thoughts get jumbled. I'm doing okay though," Charles says.

"I tried to see you."

"What? When?"

"Yesterday. But they wouldn't let me in."

"That would have been nice. I would have liked that. A real visitor. My parents were supposed to come this past weekend from Ohio but they didn't. My dad had the flu."

"Have you heard from Caroline?"

She is sorry she asked as soon she has said the words.

"Nah. She's busy. With school and field hockey and stuff."

"I've been thinking about Sarah," Grace says. "And how she must have felt out of control. Maybe even desperate."

"Yeah. I think drugs made her do things that she never would have done otherwise."

"Like what?"

"Like the money borrowing. It got more and more intense, until one time I told her 'no more.' I wanted so much to help her. I didn't care about going to class or doing homework or writing papers. All I cared about was her."

"What did she do when you cut her off?"

"She looked like I had just slapped her. She was stunned. She said, 'I thought we were friends.' I felt terrible. She walked out."

"What did you do?" Grace asks.

"I shut all the shades and sat in the dark. I watched a lot of pornography on the computer. I gorged myself. Donuts in the morning, fast food in the afternoon, alcohol at night. It felt like the world was swirling. Some-times I would drive around campus looking for her, to make sure she was okay. But I never saw her."

"What about the motel?" Grace pushes ahead. "Why were you there? Why was she?"

He lets out a low sound from deep in his throat.

"Tell me," she says.

"I went to that awful motel because—I went there be-cause I wanted to kill myself. I was finally going to do it, for real this time. I took a knife and a bottle of vodka. I didn't want to do it in the condo because the manager was nice to me, so I drove around until I found that disgusting place. I checked in. I set the knife on the bedside table and started drinking. And I couldn't even do it."

"You were alone?"

"Yes."

"Charles. What happened?"

Grace hears his labored breathing.

"My cell phone rang. It was Sarah. She wanted me to pick her up."

## CHAPTER 28

Y*ou told your father that you couldn't concentrate in the dorm because of all the partying. You wanted to move away, and he made it happen. That's something he's good at. He increased your allowance by a thousand a month to cover rent. You have never been a huge fan of the beach, having to go without a shirt is reason enough, but you want to be able to say you're living large, to be able to say, "You should hang at my crib at the beach." You imagine Sarah arriving at your door and how you'll walk with her down to the water's edge at the end of the day and hold her in the sand that still hums with warmth from the sun. She hasn't come to visit yet but your hope is a dormant seed waiting for water in the dark soil. You are infinitely patient even though she is so mad at you she hasn't talked to you in weeks. Or maybe she never thinks about you at all, there's that option,* *but it just can't be, can it?*

You have never kissed a girl. Yes, there was the transaction with the prostitute that helped alleviate something for a moment, but there was never a girl who liked you, who closed her eyes and leaned her face toward yours with dreamy anticipation. You tell the guys here that there's a girl from home—blond, nice rack—who's at Ohio State and who's coming to visit soon, who's killing you, man, because there are so many hot chicks running around Emeryville. And you tell your old classmates at Hunter High, via an online post, that you have a girlfriend at Emeryville who rocks your world.

You drive your Land Rover around Campus Drive when you're supposed to be in Western Civilization discussing The Sorrows of Young Werther. *You don't see Sarah but you do see Amy waiting for the shuttle and she flags you down. You slow to a stop and quickly eject a Sade CD, winging it into the backseat, and you turn on the rap station.*

"Hey, Raggatt," Amy says. "Can you drop me off at the mall? I need to get a birthday present for Megan."

"Sure, no problem," you say, as you always do. She gets in and slouches down in the seat. "Did you change your hair?" you ask.

Her natural red has been bleached. She flips the ends between her fingers.

"For fun," she says.

But she's clearly self-conscious about it. It's too obvious,

too out of character. You recognize something familiar in Amy.
She watches the popular girls with a hunger akin to lust.

"Do you mind?" she asks, reaching for the radio.

She turns it up and you can feel the bass in your feet.

"Where have you been, anyway?" she yells.

"I moved to the beach," you say. "I have a sweet setup.
You should come hang out some time."

"That's cool," she says, nodding, knowing she never will
because you have already been deemed uncool and she can't
risk it. Using you is fine and easily explained away, as long
as she doesn't get caught being your friend. "So John gets a
single then?"

"Yeah, I guess."

You underestimated your roommate. You thought he
was a math nerd but he found a pretty girlfriend within
weeks. You never get it right.

"Lucky bastard," she says, turning down the music a
little. "I guess that means no more happy hours."

She smiles wanly since you both know people stopped
wanting to come to your room. Even free alcohol wasn't
enough to lure them in.

"Rush starts next week," she says, trying to sound upbeat, but her voice betrays her anxiety.

Amy will want to get into Pi Phi but will probably have
to settle for a sorority where the girls are nice but not as hot
or popular.

"Good luck," you say.

The SAEs still chant "Ra-ggatt, Ra-ggatt" when you roll a keg in from your car or when they fake-box with you, but at some point you realized that you weren't one of them, just the butt of their jokes, so you won't humiliate yourself further by trying to become official. You tell them you'll help with hazing and they say, "Yeah you will, Raggatt," and laugh and give you high fives.

"Which side do you want?" you ask, pulling into the mall parking lot.

You have lost your desire to even feign jocularity.

"In front of Macy's is good," Amy says, checking her lip gloss in her compact mirror.

You feel pressure in your temples and heaviness in your limbs. Your mouth is too rubbery-limp to smile.

"Thanks for the lift," she says, hopping out. "See you at casino night on Friday?"

You nod and wave, your eyes behind your sunglasses blurring out of focus.

You drive back to the dark, bare-walled condo where your clothes are still in garbage bags and your computer is on the floor and your TV takes up one whole wall, like a giant mouth waiting to swallow you up. Your mother sent you a box of things for the kitchen, which you haven't opened. It sits on the counter with your unused textbooks. You crawl into the corner of your bedroom.

You have been asleep for hours when a door slamming in the

parking lot startles you awake. It's dark and you are on the floor, your head under the bed. You had your chance with Sarah and you blew it.

"I thought we were friends," she said.

Maybe the money was not what made her say it. Maybe you really did hurt her feelings. Maybe it is you who is the jerk.

You skulk over to the computer and go to a bestiality website where you have gone before but it doesn't do much for you. You try other porn sites but the colors and images flash without much effect. You might as well be dead, you think, and then you think it again, over and over: you might as well be dead. It could be a lot better than all this. It might even be nice.

In the kitchen you open the box from your mom. There is no note. There is a silverware organizer, six mugs, some dish towels, a nonstick frying pan, a set of knives in a wooden holder. Your parents were going to help you move but something came up and they stayed home. You dump the contents of the box into the sink, breaking two of the mugs.

You look through the slats of your blinds at the dark and empty backyard and the barbecue pit that no one uses. You slump down to the kitchen floor—gravity is too strong a force to combat—and you wonder how long it would take someone to find you if you never moved again. But then you think of the knives, a serrated one for bread, a large one for chopping, a paring knife, and the small one with the curved tip to separate meat from bone.

The hotels in town are too nice or too busy, so it takes a while to find the right location, an isolated, decaying place that will take you in and leave you alone. You find the Econo Lodge way out in Hickton.

Underneath the smell of synthetic air freshener, the room is dank with mildew. Next to the bed you place the knife and a bottle of Stoli, and you pick up the phone to call Caroline one last time, but you're afraid one of your parents might answer so you don't. You turn on the TV to an old repeat of Law & Order *and drink as much vodka as you can before it starts to come back up. When the show ends, you stare at the pale undersides of your wrists and imagine the knife going in, popping through the skin, vertical lines from your hands up to your elbows. You want to prolong it, that moment when you first press the blade in. The guy at the counter was nice so you think you will do it in the bathtub to make cleanup easier. You doze.*

When your cell phone rings and jerks you awake, you see it's 1:02 a.m. on the clock radio and you scramble for your phone, lost within the folds of the slithery, stiff bedspread. Your heart is uncontainable. The name on the caller ID gives you the shock of your life.

"Sarah." Your voice cracks.

"Hey."

"Hey, hi, how are you? I thought you hated me."

"Of course I don't hate you." There is a staticky pause. *"Could you come get me? So we can talk?"*

"Um, yeah. Totally," you say.

You know you sound too eager and loud but you can't help it. Sarah Shafer has said she needs to see you. You are not crazy. You leave the knife and the bottle and pull the flimsy door behind you.

You find her outside the dorm where she sits on the curb in the dark. She looks a little burned-out in her sweatpants and old T-shirt, her hair disheveled, her face gaunt, but she's still pretty in a way that buoys your spirit. When she gets in the car she doesn't look at you but that's okay, because she's really there.

"Are you okay?" you ask.

"Have you ever taken GHB?" she asks, tapping her finger against the window.

"No, I don't think so," you say.

"It's kind of cool, I guess," she says with an unfamiliar spaciness. *"A little mellow for my taste."* She laughs.

You drive for a while and then you say, *"When you called I was in a motel room. I was going to kill myself."*

"What?" she turns to look at you in the red glow of the stoplight. *"Shit, Charles. You poor thing."*

You shrug, but you want to weep at her show of concern.

"You have to always think about how awful it would be for your parents, you know," she says. *"Even when there don't*

seem to be any options left." She takes her hair and ties it in a knot on top of her head but it quickly falls. "Let's go there," she says. "To the motel."

You will do anything for this girl.

"Sit next to me," she says, patting her hand on the bed. She picks up the knife and traces the blade across her fingertip. She sets it down on the bedside table. "Come here," she says with a soft purr, her eyelids heavy.

You feel so light, weightless, and amazed by what is happening that for an instant you think you might already be dead. Her hand, small and soft, is on yours. It pulses. She seems a little out of it, a different kind of Sarah, but right now, you don't give a shit. You want to take in every detail. The lock of hair that has slipped from behind her ear, the bitten-down cuticles, the yellow shadow of a bruise on her slender forearm. Your life has led to this moment and you want to slow it down, wrap it around you, feel its soft underbelly.

"You are so beautiful," you say.

She half-laughs and shakes her head.

"Don't," she says, with a dryness you don't expect.

"Sarah," you say, your voice trembling.

She pets your arm.

"Shh," she says.

She takes off her shirt, just like that, and straddles you, and there is her lovely warm skin inches from your face. She grabs the bottle and drinks, then kisses you, her lips warm and boozy.

It lasts no more than a few minutes, Sarah rushing you forward, you trying to hold it in, awkwardness you might have feared bulldozed over by your want and incredulity. There is something mechanical in Sarah's actions, something listless in her eyes that you ignore, knowing it is a projection of your nerves.

When you are inside, you lose your breath. You let yourself believe that you have found the person who can solder all these parts of yourself into a whole. That song she likes floods your head in full stereo, "Sarah, oh Sarah, loving you is the one thing I will never regret." You grin like a mad hyena, and let go

You are afloat in the afterglow, so happy you want to burst.

"I love you," you say, opening your eyes and turning to her.

Sarah sits up and pulls on her shirt. She rubs her face, then her nose. Her hand shakes.

"So the money?" she asks quietly.

"What?" you ask, propping yourself up on your elbows, your smile fading as the words form their meaning.

Your paunch is white and puckered. You are turning back into yourself.

"Please, Charles. Don't make it harder than it already

is. I don't know who else to turn to."

Your mind races and skips, lost in thorny branches. You feel your fragile porcelain heart start to crack and fall away, until there is nothing left but rage, black and shiny-smooth like obsidian.

"You got what you wanted," she says, trying to smile to make it seem less brutal, but that only makes it worse.

She pulls on her underwear.

You reach for her but she scoots away to the edge of the bed.

"Sarah," you say. She doesn't answer. "I thought…" but you can't finish because it is such a tired refrain: once again, you are the fool.

You sit up. Your penis lolls to one side, deflated and pink.

And there it is, that cool glint of metal from the bedside table, answering a question you haven't yet asked. The knife is in your hand then and you press the blade into your neck.

"I'll do it," you say, through clenched teeth.

She looks at you and through drugged, half-closed eyes says, "Come on, Charles, don't be so dramatic. I just need the money."

You are crying now, furious, devastated.

You lunge at her and take her to the floor with your bloated girth. She slaps at you with her free hand, a frenzied, helpless animal, but she doesn't call out or scream, not quite believing the danger that pushes through your every cell.

"You fucking lunatic," she spits from underneath you.

"Get the fuck off me."

The knife is still in your hand and you bring it down to stop it all. Everything pours from you into the violence of the knife in your hand. The blade goes in with little resistance, right between her ribs. Sarah's expression is shock and confusion, there is no time for fear. You know you hit her heart. She grunts, gasps, her flailing feet hitting the bed frame. You smell her blood before you even see it. Her eyes stay open; they are tunnels of vacancy. Her escaping breath, a sibilant hiss. You bring the knife down again, halfheartedly, losing will on the way down, redundantly, because she is already dead.

It is quiet. And you are alone. You lay your heavy head on the dead girl's still and bloody chest.

In the fluorescent light, the blood on your hands looks purple. You have blood on your face, in your ear. The knife is on the floor, but you don't have the guts to kill yourself, even now.

You have split in two.

You wash your arms, your face, your hair, your chest, the knife, with the little tan bar of soap, bathing the shower in pink and red. You scald yourself with the hottest water possible but it is not hot enough to burn you clean. You dry yourself and find your clothes, discarded with such abandon so little time ago.

There are garbage bags and packing tape in your car,

left over from your move out of the dorm. You retrieve them. The night is empty. You are not there. You can't even blink your eyes. You fold Sarah's slender, unwieldy body in on itself without looking at her face, bending her knees flat to her thighs, taping her arms around her knees, binding her into a compact form, her hair getting caught in the tape. You pull a bag over her, her body pressing against the plastic. You sheathe it with another bag and then another and another, wrapping it in more tape like a grisly Christo project. You carry the bundle through the dark parking lot to the back of your car.

In the now-empty room, there is a glistening amoeba stain of blood on the carpet. You soak it up as best as you can with the threadbare hotel towels. You make the bed. You find a drop of dried blood on the sink, which you frantically wipe off with the hem of your shirt. There's a smear of blood on the cuff of your jeans.

When you check out you manage to make your voice even and uninteresting, pleasant enough, apologizing to the guy for staining the carpet and telling him to charge any cleaning to your card. You don't meet his eyes, so he can't see the wilderness beneath the surface. You drop a garbage bag with the bloody towels, her cell phone, and the rest of her clothes in a dumpster.

# # #

It feels like your brain has been taken out and knocked around before being returned to your skull. Your eyes ache.

You ignore what you did because it couldn't really have happened. You stare at snow on the TV for ten hours straight. You drive around for days and forget there is a body in your car, even giving Amy a ride to the train station, even commenting on how weird it is that Sarah still hasn't turned up, and apologizing for the bad smell in the car that's maybe from when you hit a skunk. You are scared to look at your face in the mirror, afraid of what it might reveal. Your mind has broken apart like a green tree branch, fibrous and wet. The world warbles, and you move numbly through it in a stupor, reduced to a pile of jagged rubble deep inside.

# # #

A week has passed. You bury Sarah in the middle of the night, quietly digging in the sparse grass and sandy soil fifteen feet from your window.

You sleep for two feverish days, and then you pick up the phone and tell them where to find you.

## CHAPTER 29

And now Grace knows too much. The seams she pried open for a glimpse inside have all come undone, leaving a large gaping hole. She feels heavy and used up. Now it's the face of Sarah she sees when she closes her eyes, those brown eyes, startled, lacking any understanding that such a thing could happen to her. Those rich maple eyes like Callie's.

There has always been something else about her sister's death, casting an inky shadow. It was quickly deposited away, stuffed down, buried deep. Unfathomable, it became maybe not true. It was easier to believe the story that everyone else knew.

But something has irrevocably shifted in Grace and what was sealed is breaking open. She doesn't have enough fingers to stop the leaks, springing up all over her memory. She is running to where she has been running away from. She finds her car and hurtles toward home.

She remembers the way her mother climbed the stairs after the funeral, how she gripped the banister, leaning her weight with each step, so slowly, as if overnight she'd become an arthritic old woman.

People came and went with Tupperware casseroles and condolences. They spoke hushed words of sympathy, especially to her mother, whom the ladies hijacked away to quiet corners. Grace moved around from room to room, watching, unseen.

"He's much too old to be driving."

"He almost hit the Millers' dog last week."

"A tragedy."

"Do you want to play doubles Tuesday? Margaret can't make it."

"What was she doing in the street? She knew better."

"Susan is holding it together remarkably well."

"She tripped while the girls were playing. That cute little Callie."

"Did you hear that Gracie saw it happen? Just awful."

"Have you seen the monstrosity they're building over on Pine?"

"Oh that poor woman. I just can't imagine."

Grace stayed home from school for a week and in that time she rarely saw her mother or her father. She ate cereal and crackers and cheese. She wandered in the woods and slept on the couch, unable to breathe next to Callie's empty room, with the stuffed elephant she'd named Herbert, the folders of her penny collection, a ballerina jewelry box that their grandmother had sent for Callie's sixth birthday, filled with gumball machine jewelry and three baby teeth. The smell of her pillow.

###

Grace pulls into a rest stop somewhere in the leafy mountains midway through Pennsylvania and lays her head against the sun-hot steering wheel. When she looks up, she sees three barefooted, grubby children tumble out of the back of a rusty van and run to the little patch of grass in front of her car. The two older children, boys, take the feet and hands of the little girl and swing her like a hammock, higher and higher, almost all the way around. Her screams of delight quickly turn into frightened pleas for release. The boys keep going, with a quick backward glance to make sure their father is not watching, as the girl starts to cry.

"Promise you'll do whatever we tell you to do," the older boy says.

"And that you won't tell, you brat," says the other.

She relents.

They let her down roughly onto the grass and walk away, laughing, back toward the van.

They don't give her another thought, not hearing her

little feet padding across the ground, not sensing her ferocious anger, not believing that she could attack on her own. She is running with everything in her small body and she comes up behind her unsuspecting brother, the one closer to her in age, the one with whom she's better matched in size, her elbows bent, her hands open for action, and with all her might, she shoves him, sending him skidding until he falls face-first onto the asphalt of the parking lot, his chin and cheek grated bloody by the gravel.

In the moment that Mr. Jablonski's car appeared around the corner in front of their house, Grace bent her arms just like that little girl did, and she came at Callie, fueled by her own agency and power, somehow unable to see past the allure of the thrust to what would actually happen, to the devastating effect, and she pushed. She shoved Callie into the street, in front of the oncoming car.

Two hours later, Grace is still at the rest stop, clutching the wheel with aching fingers. Shallow-breathed and sunburned, she sits, her body pitched forward, unable to start the car, unable to focus her eyes. A loud knock on her window shakes her. At first she thinks it's the police who've come to arrest her. But it's only a park service worker.

"You all right?" he asks as she rolls down the window.

"Um, yeah," she says, clearing her throat. "Yes."

"I was here a couple hours ago and when I came back you were still in the same position, like you'd been frozen."

"I needed to rest a little," she says. "I'm going to get going now."

She swipes her hair from her face and adjusts in the seat.

"Okay then," he says. He steps back but then comes forward again. "You sure you're all right? You look like you seen a ghost."

"I'm fine," she says, fumbling with the keys already in the ignition. "Thanks."

"Drive safe," he says with a little nod.

## CHAPTER 30

It's after two a.m. when Grace turns onto Woodland. The houses are all tucked in on this still summer night, the lawns in the moonlight cropped close and watered to lushness. Crickets trill their intermittent night call. Flags are unfurled on porch eaves for the Fourth of July weekend.

When Grace reaches the driveway, it's all she can do not to make a U-turn. But with every familiar detail—the pewter 3 of their address slightly askew on the gatepost, the patch of lawn near the base of the oak that never fills in no matter how much her father tends to it, the deep furrow in the driveway that would catch her roller skates if she hit it at the wrong angle—she knows that this is the only path she has left.

The house is dark except for the lantern flickering in front. Grace leans into her car door and presses it closed.

The night is crisp with green. She takes off her shoes and steps along the cool flagstone path up to the house, trying each door. Around the back, the ground slick with dew, an animal dashes into the woods at her approach. She goes to the rarely used back door that her mother always forgets to lock and lets herself in.

She moves up the stairs toward her old room, but then she hears a cough. She goes back down. Her father is asleep in his study, his ankles crossed on the ottoman, slouched in the chair that is as much a part of him as his golf swing. The moon shines near-full through the front window, shrouding the room in dusty light. Despite the imprint of age and slackness from the stroke, he is still handsome. His white hair is a sparse halo. His slippered feet twitch in sleep.

"Dad," Grace whispers. "Daddy."

She goes to him and shakes his foot.

"Oh. Hi," he says, awakening, like her appearance in his dark office is the most normal thing.

He scrunches his face and then registers whom he's talking to.

"Grace."

"Are you awake?" she asks.

"Uh-huh."

"I have to tell you something."

He straightens up a little in his seat.

"What are you doing here? I thought you went back

to New York," he says.

"I did something terrible," she says.

She can no longer hold herself up. She sinks to her knees next to him.

He squints at her.

"It's late. I must have fallen asleep."

He looks at his watch but can't read it in the dark.

"I did it," she says.

"You did what?" he asks. "Whatever it is, it can't be that bad."

"Callie."

"Come now, Grace. You'll feel better in the morning."

"It was my fault." Her voice is someone else's, low and parched and sober.

His eyes are glossy in the low light. He puts his feet on the floor and sits forward, hands on his knees, preparing to stand. But she grasps onto his arm and won't let him. He settles back. She waits in the hallucinatory semi-darkness. She feels like she is melting.

"You were just a child," he says. He speaks slowly, his speech still thickened. "It was a terrible accident."

"No, it wasn't, Dad."

"Let's not talk about it," he says. He places his palm gently on her head. "Go on up to bed."

"She didn't trip."

"I remember that day so well. You in your shirt with the big cherries on it."

He smiles and meets her eyes.

"I'm telling you," she says. "I pushed Callie into the street," she says.

"No you didn't, Grace. She lost her balance and she fell."

"I pushed her."

The first waking birds twitter just outside the window. Her father looks down at her upturned face, worn and raw, and then turns away to the window, up at the moon. He rubs his bristled chin. He shakes his head. He reaches behind the chair for a stashed bottle of bourbon and opens it, drinking fast, before putting the cork back in.

And then, finally, he says softly, "I saw what happened."

Grace feels like she can't get enough air.

"You saw?" Her words are hoarse.

"I loved watching you girls play." He takes a breath, steadying himself. "My hands were on the window to open it, to tell you to move away from the street. Everything seemed to just slow down." He coughs and tries to clear his voice. "The sound of those car brakes."

His hand reaches to his tremulous lips.

"I can still hear that awful sound," he says.

Grace loved that shirt. She'd gotten it earlier in the summer at the Spring Blossom Festival—the flea-bitten carnival manned by long-haired, bearded men in coveralls that rolled into the nearby town of Maple Hill every year. She poured her saved-up allowance into the rigged games, particularly intent on the one where she tossed rings to catch the top of milk bottles. She played until she won. Her prize was a choice between a stuffed duck, a feathered roach clip that she didn't know the use of, and a cherry T-shirt. A well-earned reward.

Callie coveted the shirt, and that August day Grace not only discovered her wearing it, but also saw grape juice spilled on the front. She demanded Callie take it off. Her sister refused. They were about the same size—Grace a little taller, Callie a little stronger—and when they went at it, they were pretty well matched. Grace wrestled her down, trying to get the shirt over her head until her mother discovered them and restored order. Grace got her shirt back, and promptly put it on. They continued the battle on the floor of the living room over a game of Monopoly, which soon escalated to accusations over houses and hotels and mis-moves.

"Enough," her mother said.

Something had happened the night before with her parents. They didn't seem to be speaking that day. He, holed away in his study, and she, on her fifth cup of coffee, looked tired and drawn. Grace had remembered doors slamming after she was already in bed, some vitriolic exchanges downstairs.

"Outside. Both of you," her mother said. "I do not

want to hear a peep or see a hair on your heads until lunchtime. Do you hear me? Grace, would you please try to set a good example for your sister?"

Callie scrambled to the den. Their dad's face was pale and bloated.

"Daddy, come outside," Callie said, pulling his hand, the parental discord and his raging hangover unknown to her. "Let's play tag. Come on, you promised."

He smiled at her and tugged on her hair. Grace stood back in the doorway.

"Sorry, sweetie, not today. Your dad needs some quiet time. I have a headache."

He stirred his Bloody Mary with his finger.

"Please, please, please?"

"Come on, Callie," Grace said. "Stop being such a pest."

Outside the day was steaming up, an old-fashioned Midwest summer. They'd learned in school how the cicadas this year were from a special brood, underground for seventeen years, and how large numbers of them would blanket the area. The cicadas were there all right, buzzing and whining, big-bodied and everpresent, weighing down tree branches, clogging up the grills of cars. In bare feet, the girls had to be careful not to step on the molted shells.

"You're It," Callie said.

"You can't play tag with two people," Grace said.

"Let's play kickball."

Grace rolled her eyes.

"No."

"Let's play Charlie's Angels."

"That's not a game."

"Let's play...I am the queen and you are my servant."

Her laugh was honey-sweet. They skipped across the lawn. Grace did a cartwheel, and then Callie did one. Grace picked errant dandelions. Callie taunted the Millers' Irish setter, who rooted around the ivy across the street.

"Come here, Rusty, come on you old dumb dog," Callie sang out between her hands. "Hey, how about Marco Polo?"

"You can't play that with two people either. There's no point," Grace said. But then she relented, because what else was there to do? "Not It."

Callie closed her eyes and held out her hands.

"Marco."

"Polo."

"Marco."

"Polo."

Callie moved right to Grace with some overacted double-backs.

"Close your eyes, Callie. I can see your eyeballs."

She laughed.

"They're closed! Okay, now they're closed. Marco."

"Polo."

They were near the road. Callie moved in her direction, but Grace quietly ran around behind her.

"Marco."

Grace heard tires on the sticky, hot pavement. The impulse was whip-quick. She didn't think about her sister dying. She just saw her in a perfect, unsuspecting position.

"Polo!"

Grace's hands hit Callie's bony girl-back and her sister's head jerked and the toe of her sneaker caught the edge of the asphalt and she flew headfirst into the street and then the old wood-paneled cinnamon-colored car was upon her and scooped her up—the thud of the body against the car and the screech of brakes and the finality of crushed glass as Callie bounced up into the windshield.

Her sister's face was untouched, and at first, Grace thought she was going to climb down and tell on her. But then her eyes didn't move and there was blood, as if on time-delay, pouring from her head. Mr. Jablonski was making choking sounds and moans, reaching for Callie but then pulling his hands back. Her father appeared. Her mother. Dr. Miller ran toward them. Another neighbor called an ambulance.

Screams and screams and screams.

Grace was frozen, terrified. She wanted to believe what her dad was saying. Callie fell. It was an accident. Go inside, go inside.

"You never said anything," Grace says.

The tears run in rivulets and hang off her chin.

"What was there to say?" her father says. "I didn't want to make it real. I thought you might forget. I don't know. Maybe it was the wrong thing."

"I killed her." The words are acid on her tongue.

"No, you didn't," he says wearily. "That's not what I saw. You were a child playing a game. It was an awful mistake."

She crawls into his lap. She cries and cries until, for the moment, she is empty.

"Grace," he says, patting her hand, "it doesn't matter anymore. It was so very long ago."

They sit in silence and the minutes linger on. His eyes flutter closed. She takes her father's hand and holds it against her cheek.

"You're not going to climb back up into the tree, are you?" he asks.

# # #

In the morning, Grace finds her dad at the kitchen table drinking coffee with an unsteady hand. He is momentarily confused by her presence, but then something clicks and he goes back to reading the paper. He doesn't say anything about last night and she knows he will never mention it again. Maybe he thought it was a dream or maybe he has forgotten. Maybe he knows there is nothing else to say.

"There's more coffee," he says.

"Thanks," she says, pouring herself some. "Have you gotten all your slides sorted out?"

"Almost," he says, smiling a little. "Maybe next time we'll have a show."

"I'd like that," she says.

He goes back to reading.

"I better go say hi to Mom."

"In her tomatoes," he says without looking up.

The plants are now staked and three feet tall, bent with the weight of their green yield. Her mother kneels between rows and all Grace can see is the back of her pertly bobbed hair.

"Nice plants," Grace says.

"Gracie," her mother says, rising from the dirt. "You nearly gave me a heart attack."

"Surprise," Grace says.

Her mother takes off her gloves and hugs her daughter daintily, and Grace is once again reminded of her fragility, the smaller she seems each time she sees her. Her mother touches the purple rim of Grace's eye but doesn't say anything about it.

"What's the occasion? Not that you need one to come home."

"Nothing, really. I just felt like it."

Grace sips her coffee.

"Are you sure everything's all right?" her mother says,

narrowing her eyes as if to better see inside her daughter's inscrutable heart.

Grace nods.

She knows her mother wants to say, "You are thirty-five years old, Grace. What are you doing with your life?" But instead she tucks a lock of hair behind her daughter's ear.

"I know why you're here," her mother says, wagging her finger.

"You do?"

"You couldn't bear to miss the fireworks."

"Right," Grace says, and smiles. "You got me."

"We'll leave here around 8:30. You can make the deviled eggs."

⚓ ⚓ ⚓

Dear Charles,

I think that I understand now, as much as I am able to. Whatever happens with the trial, know that I believe in the *you* that I have come to know.

I went home again to Cleveland to see my parents. Tonight we are going to watch fireworks from the golf course of the country club like we haven't done since my sister was alive, and we will remember how it used to be. But we might also reconcile ourselves to how it has turned out and be okay with that. We shall see.

Be well, Charles.

Your friend,

Grace

♯ ♯ ♯

They situate themselves on the velvet green of the sixth
hole of the club course, the air soft and warm, the twilight
a violet haze behind the trees. They are quiet and gentle
with each other, passing the food between them. Children
run around, antsy to be awed. Harvey Chenowith's rau-
cous laughter cuts through the growing darkness.

When the fireworks start, the three of them look up,
lost in thought and light. Grace pulls the little flag out of
her cupcake and licks the frosting as the lights twirl and
dance in the sky. In the dappled reflection of the explo-
sions, she steals a glance at her parents' upturned faces.

The finale is never enough, never quenching—no matter
how many colors, how expansive the cascading lights,
how intricate the designs, how loud the booms and whistles, how quick the successions, it always leaves Grace
wanting, not quite satisfied. But as the family walks away,
she holding onto her father's arm and her mother taking
his other hand, stepping carefully in the sultry dark toward the lights of the clubhouse, Grace feels the
possibility of a tenuous repose.

———

September 15, 2003. Charles Raggatt, 19, of Hunter, OH, fidgeted and twitched his head during a brief court proceeding before Nassau County Court Judge Richard Castiglione. Raggatt told the judge he understood the ramifications of entering a felony guilty plea.

———

## CHAPTER 31

Just before jury selection was scheduled to begin, Charles made a deal with the prosecutors to plead guilty to one count of second degree murder for a lesser sentence. In the note about it in the *Post*, his defense attorney said the Raggatts had not attended the proceeding because of a previous commitment. Sarah's parents sat stoically in the front row of the courtroom.

Grace drives out to Long Island to attend the sentencing hearing, to see Charles in person. The day is warm but not stifling, incongruously beautiful for the proceedings. Inside the drab courtroom the windows are open wide and a fan blasts above the judge's bench. The lawyers from both sides are here, and in the gallery there are a couple of reporters. Sarah's parents, seated in the front row, stare straight ahead with swollen, glassy eyes. The

Raggatts are absent once again. One of the bailiffs fans herself with an empty legal folder.

There is a small hush when Charles, in prison orange and white sneakers without laces, is brought in. His body looks deflated from when she first saw him months ago. Above all, Grace is struck by his youth in a way that she had lost sight of. He is just a teenager, not even fully formed. She aches at the sight of him, unable, in the end, to do anything for him.

He does not look up from the floor as he is led to the defense table. She thought he might look for her, but as far as he knows, she could be anyone. Once seated, he hangs his head and closes his eyes.

The judge sentences him to twenty-five years to life, which gives Charles the possibility of parole when he is forty-five years old.

Charles, never lifting his eyes, apologizes to Sarah's parents in a stilted, incoherent speech. He is nervous and rambling, unable to make the words mean all the sorrow he wants to communicate. He tries to wipe his tears with his shoulder. Her parents refuse to look at him, her mother facing the window as he talks, her father watching the clock. When Charles stops making sense altogether, the judge orders him to wrap it up.

"In the end I have destroyed a lot of lives," Charles mutters, his eyes cast downward, "and what more is there to say?"

He looks up briefly with faraway, mournful eyes, as if seeking out the horizon. There is silence, a cough, a jangle of keys. Soft cries from Sarah's mother. Grace tries to catch Charles's gaze but comes up empty.

# # #

The following day Grace goes back to the Mineola jail, this time during visiting hours. Now that there is no trial to prepare for, the restrictions on Charles have been lifted. He will be transferred within the week to a prison upstate. The officers on duty do not recognize her and she passes through metal detectors and pea green hallways to a windowless room lined with vending machines. It is sparsely occupied by men in orange who murmur in low tones to their women, most of whom have dressed up in low-cut tops and thigh-high skirts. One of them eyes Grace's sundress with derision. In a room off to the side, a heavily tattooed man with a pointy mustache leans his chair back across from his harried, court-appointed lawyer.

It's ten minutes before Charles is brought in, his wrists manacled together in front. He trudges along behind the corrections officer, led like a mule.

"Hi," she says.

He looks up slowly, moving like he is underwater.

"Oh," he says. "Hi."

She rises and holds out her hand.

"I'm Grace," she says.

His face goes soft and then he reaches out to her with

his clumsy, cuffed hands. She looks at those hands and inwardly retracts, fearing what they have done. But then she takes them in hers, and the feeling fades.

They sit across from each other at a plastic table.

"You're Grace," he says, with a spreading smile. "I'm Charles Raggatt."

"I know," she says.

"It's nice to meet you," he says. "I mean in person. I'm sorry I haven't called."

He looks away, as if she might scold him.

"That's okay," she says. "You've had a lot going on."

He stares off, then jerks his head to dislodge the thoughts.

"How are you feeling?" she asks.

"It's unforgivable, what I did," he says, his face contorting, crumbling.

She reaches out her hand and touches his arm to bring him back.

"Thank you," she says. "For all that you told me."

For the briefest moment, his doughy face falls away and before her is a sweet little boy, a slight blush to his cheeks, a brightness for having pleased. But it swiftly dims.

"Do you want something from the vending machines?" she asks.

"Okay," he says. "I like the ice cream sandwiches."

When she returns, he seems to have regained some

clarity of thought. He looks more self-possessed, more present. He unwraps his ice cream and takes a bite, then another, chewing quietly.

"Did you go on field trips to Severance Hall as a kid?" he asks.

"I did," she says, "and I usually fell asleep."

"I was the only one who ever seemed to like it. I would close my eyes and then the music started and I wouldn't think of anything else. That was heaven for me."

She smiles.

"Yesterday I was thinking that maybe there's accumulation that can happen with good things. That they can add up to counteract the bad."

"That's a nice way to think about it," she says.

"I tend to forget the good stuff."

"I do, too."

"Grace, it's really you."

She laughs a little.

"It's really me."

"It's weird we're just meeting now."

He traces an ink stain on the table with his finger.

"Hey, I realized the other day that you never told me what happened to your sister. How she died."

His handcuffed hands rest in a quiet heap on the table.

"She was hit by a car," Grace says.

"Oh," he says. "That's too bad."

Something flickers in his eyes. Maybe he knows better than anyone that there is no end to what goes unsaid.

"So," she says, fidgeting with her visitor's pass. "When are you moving?"

"Not long now," he says. His eyes glaze over. "They got me into a good place I think. Where I can get some counseling or something. I can thank my lawyer for that. It's up in the northern part of New York. Not that far from Canada."

Grace thinks that in some sense Charles is relieved to be no longer in control, to do only as he is told, shorn of responsibility for what he is and what he is capable of.

"That's good, Charles," she says, palming her keys in her pocket, suddenly feeling the need to go, to extricate herself from the terrible inelegance of meeting for the first and last time.

"What are you going to do now?" he asks.

"I don't know," she says. "Go back to my regular life, I guess."

He nods and nods, slightly rocking in his chair.

"Are you disappointed?" he asks, his face a desert of limitless need.

She doesn't know whether he means in him, in his guilty plea, in the whole affair.

"No," she says emphatically. "Not in the slightest."

He smiles, first shyly, then with irrepressible pleasure.

# # #

Grace drives out to the town of Nutley, New Jersey, looking for the grave of Sarah Shafer. She has given the girl unpardonably little thought during all of this, and for that she is sorry. It takes her all afternoon, but in the third cemetery she finds it, under a downy shroud of new grass, with a freshly incised, rose-colored granite headstone.

Beloved daughter and sister.

Grace leaves a bouquet of peonies.

#

Grace's seat at Chances is just as she left it. Jimmy has lost a little weight and he beams when she compliments him on it.

The wine goes down too smoothly.

"You're moving?" Jimmy asks, wide-eyed, as he pours her another.

"Don't worry," she says, "I'd never leave you. I'm only going three blocks away."

"Thank God," he says. "For a minute there I thought I'd been dumped."

The best part about the new apartment is the view. Grace will be able to see all the way out to the Statue of Liberty from her kitchen. She drinks her wine down fast and slides her glass down the bar to Jimmy.

"One more," she says.

"Gracie," he says. "Welcome back."

#

Dear Grace,

Thank you for coming to see me. I wish it had been under better circumstances. I'm afraid the stress of everything has taken its toll. But it was great to finally meet you face to face.

I forgot to tell you one of my new favorite quotes I found in my book. "It's better to be hated for what you are than loved for what you are not." Maybe there's something to it. I think it will be good for me to keep in mind.

I'm going away, as you know, for very many years. I admit that I've had thoughts of killing myself, particularly in the last few days. But then I remember you, and how for the first time I know what it's like to have a real friend.

Maybe when I get out, we can sit down in a café over coffee and talk as old friends who haven't seen each other in a long time. I would like that.

Yours truly,
Charles T. Raggatt

# # #

Grace is six and Callie is four, and they are with their parents, posing for a family portrait in the woods behind their house. The photographer wants the shot framed by branches, so they are all sitting in the brambles, trying to look comfortable as they slap at mosquitoes.

"Okay, why don't we try a standing one," he says.

They move out of the trees and around to the front of the house. He arranges them in a line across, with Grace and Callie in matching sailor dresses in the middle, and directs them to walk together, hand in hand, up the driveway.

Callie refuses to hold Grace's hand.

"I said I was sorry," Grace says.

Callie scowls.

Their father gets down on his haunches next to her.

"Forgiveness is in your hands," he says, glancing quickly up to his wife. "It's a powerful position to be in, you know. Grace said she was sorry, now it's up to you."

Never one to resist his charms, Callie's pout recedes and she takes her sister's hand. Her smile blooms.

"Doesn't that feel better?" he asks, tickling her protruding stomach.

They assemble and they walk. Their parents catch eyes above their heads, and then Grace turns because Callie has called her name.

Snap.

"I think that was the one, folks," the photographer says.

But none of them hear. Grace and Callie are laughing and running, tugging their parents along. The four of them are, for the briefest, sun-bleached moment, an impenetrable unit, an unbroken force moving through the world. They collapse on the lawn. The wind is light. The photographer goes to his car for a new lens.

"Can we do an airplane?" Callie asks, poking her dad as he stretches out on his back.

She recognizes a prime opportunity, knows when he's an easy target for attention giving.

Grace lies on the grass and rests her head in her mother's lap.

"Jack, your shoes," her mother says, brushing her soft palm across her Grace's forehead again and again. "You'll get her dress all dirty."

He holds his feet in the air, one at a time, and Callie wriggles off his topsiders, tossing each one out into the yard.

Callie places her belly on her father's feet. She grabs his hands. They lock eyes, she with anticipatory glee, he with dramatic flourish, and slowly, slowly, he lifts her. She holds her body straight out with childish grace, her strong little legs tensed, her toes pointed like her mother has taught her, and with shrieks of joy, up and up she goes.

But after a moment Callie quiets. She raises her eyes, and with great determination she lets go of her dad's hands, breaking away from all of them, flying on faith.

From her angle, Grace sees only girl and sky.

ACKNOWLEDGMENTS

For their unwavering support, my gratitude goes to: Alex Darrow, Jennifer Sey, the Meadows family, and the Darrow family. A special thank you to Christopher Sey for asking me the question that set this novel in motion.

I am indebted to my dear agent and advocate Elisabeth Weed, and to my insightful and encouraging editor Kate Nitze. Thanks also to Julie Burton, Dorothy Carico Smith, Melanie Mitchell, David Poindexter, and Scott Allen at MacAdam/Cage.